STONE OF FIRE

AN ARKANE THRILLER

J.F. PENN

Stone of Fire. An ARKANE Thriller (Book 1)

Copyright © Joanna (J.F.) Penn (2011, 2013, 2015, 2022). All rights reserved.

Fourth Print edition. Previously published as PENTECOST

www.JFPenn.com

ISBN Paperback: 978-1-913321-96-3
ISBN Large Print: 978-1-913321-97-0
ISBN Hardback: 978-1-913321-98-7

Requests to publish work from this book should be sent to: joanna@ CurlUpPress.com

Cover and Interior Design: JD Smith Design

Printed by Lightning Source Ltd

www.CurlUpPress.com

For Jonathan.
Growing together, but not in each other's shadow.

"When the day of Pentecost came, they were all together in one place. Suddenly a sound like the blowing of a violent wind came from heaven and filled the whole house where they were sitting.

They saw what seemed to be tongues of fire that separated and came to rest on each of them. All of them were filled with the Holy Spirit and began to speak in other tongues as the Spirit enabled them.

Everyone was filled with awe, and many wonders and miraculous signs were done by the Apostles."

Acts 2:1–4, 43

PROLOGUE

Varanasi, India. May 1.

RAIN SOAKED THE ASHES of the dead into the winding Varanasi streets as rivers of mud ran down to the holy river Ganges. Beggars shivered on the steps leading down to Manikarnika, the main burning ghat, where pyres blazed continually day and night, even as the storm raged. Bodies smoldered on stacks of firewood as the sacred flames consumed the corpses, releasing them from the suffering of repeated death and rebirth.

Sister Aruna Maria hurried down an alleyway behind the spice markets, forcing her old feet to move faster, stumbling a little as she pushed off the walls that loomed above.

She glanced behind. Those following were close. She must find somewhere to hide.

An hour ago, three men had entered the little

church tucked away inside the holy Hindu city and spoken to the caretaker of the convent. They'd asked about an ancient stone, and as Aruna Maria peeked around a pillar, she'd seen money change hands.

She'd run, not even pausing for her Bible, and headed for the anonymity of the streets. But the sadhus barely tolerated Christians, and beggars would point her direction for just a few rupees.

The men would be on her trail soon enough.

Aruna Maria pushed herself faster into the labyrinth of narrow streets. She could not fathom how they had found her after so many years, but it was time to hide the stone once more. She was a Keeper, one in a long line stretching back over two millennia, each prepared for the day when evil would come for what they protected.

Now, it seemed, they had found her.

Beneath the sound of the rain, she heard running feet closing fast. Aruna Maria clutched her soaked habit in one gnarled hand as she desperately searched for sanctuary, for some dark corner to hide in. She had run through these streets since her childhood. Surely she could outpace this evil now.

A tall figure stepped out before her, dressed all in black, emerging as a wraith from the shadows.

One of the men from the church.

She gasped and turned to flee in the opposite

direction, but another man approached from behind. The streets, so busy in the day, were now empty, the shutters closed, with no witnesses to her fate.

"Calm down, sister. I just want to talk to you."

Aruna Maria could tell the man was American by his accent. Although his words promised safety, she could see his eyes in the dim light. They shone with fanaticism, a hunger for something she and few others possessed in the world.

He reached toward her. "I know you have an Apostle's stone. Give it to me and I'll let you go."

She stood her ground, heart pounding. "Don't touch me. I'm set apart for God — and I don't know of this stone you seek."

"Oh, but you do, sister."

Muscular arms pinned her from behind, holding Aruna Maria still while the American advanced. As fear tightened around her heart, she prayed aloud with ancient words handed down by the Keepers.

High above her head, storm clouds gathered, forming a tight vortex in shades of midnight. She felt an upwelling in her spirit as her words ran together, strange tongues transforming her voice as she called to God in the language of the angels.

The American gripped her throat, forcing her head back and silencing her prayers. With the other hand, he found the thin cord in the folds of her habit and lifted the stone out and over her head.

As rain lashed down, the American gazed at the stone in his palm, its roughly carved whorls set in a deeper grey.

"This is what I've been searching for, sister. Now tell me what it can do." He released his grip on her throat.

Aruna Maria looked up into the approaching storm and prayed once more, her words stronger now. God would hear her as he had heard the cries of the faithful since the days of Abraham.

Thunder rolled across the sky, and lightning crashed. Fire lit up the heavens above and flashed down to earth as if to strike the heathen.

The American slapped her face.

Her head snapped sideways and the stinging blow made Aruna Maria reel and spin — but she held her ground.

"Tell me how to use it," he demanded. "I must know."

She heard the threat in his voice, and a deep calm washed over her. Was this how the blessed martyrs felt when they faced death?

"The power of the stones was sent by God at Pentecost and forged in the blood of martyrs in the first century. The power will surge once more if the stones of the Apostles are gathered together. But they are lost to time and history. The Keepers were scattered and none of us know of the others. You will never find what you seek."

The American roared, his rage echoed by the violence of the storm.

He threw Aruna Maria down into the mud of the alleyway and kicked her old body again and again, his boots crushing the breath from her.

Aruna Maria looked up into the heart of the storm and, as she sank into blackness, she saw a pillar of fire coming down from heaven.

When she came to, Aruna Maria couldn't move, she couldn't see.

She tried to scream, but her throat was blocked, her body paralyzed.

She could barely breathe, but a small amount of air seeped through the bindings that wrapped her, just keeping her alive. Panic overwhelmed her as she gasped for breath on the edge of consciousness.

The American had taken the stone. She had failed in her sacred duty. Perhaps she deserved whatever fate was coming, for God had surely turned His face away that day.

She lay flat on her back, carried on a stretcher,

and the sound of chanting filled the air. Aruna Maria inhaled sharply as she realized what it was.

The death chant of Shiva.

It was customary to burn the dead as soon as possible after death and the American would cover his tracks by getting rid of her body. He must have paid for a quick burning amongst the many genuine dead on Manikarnika ghat.

Aruna Maria struggled against her bonds. The ghats were so close. She would soon be on a pyre, burning alive — watched by the tourists who came to gawp at the spectacle every night from boats on the Ganges.

This place existed for death. Not just the funeral pyres, but also the bodies in the river, weighed down by stones. The corpses often surfaced on the east bank of the river, rotting in the sun, eaten by carrion birds. The tourists were unaware of the bodies swaying in the current below their boats — and they were unaware of the living flesh about to be burned alive before them.

Aruna Maria's heart pounded as she smelled the pungent smoke of the fires and the heavy scent of marigolds that draped the corpses to hide the stench of death. She felt the shock of cold water as the Dalit — once known as the Untouchable caste — dipped her stretcher into the sacred river. As they laid her on the pyre, Aruna Maria prayed desperately — but there was no answer from on high.

The fire crackled to life.

Flames licked her skin through the wrappings.

Her prayers turned to screams as her throat burned through, silencing her before she died.

The American stood by the pyre, gazing into the flames as the body of the nun crisped and charred. His fingers rose to touch the stone around his neck, then he turned and faded into the alleyways of night. He would find the other stones — at any price.

BREAKING NEWS

Extract from *The Times of India*, May 2.

A violent storm rocked Varanasi last night, with lightning igniting fires across the city even in heavy rain. Witnesses saw balls of lightning, forked flame, and a pillar of fire above Manikarnika ghat on the banks of the Ganges. Scientists cannot explain how the fires burned so fiercely in monsoon conditions.

"It was as if a djinn whirled in our midst," said Rajiv Gupta, a local tradesman.

Miracles were reported at the time of the pillar of fire. Beggars living on the edges of the ghat claim to be healed of various diseases and one man allegedly regained his sight after twenty years of blindness. Hindu priests and the police are investigating the claims, reportedly attributing them to mass hysteria associated with the violent storm.

CHAPTER 1

Oxford, England. May 18

MORGAN SIERRA SAT AT her desk, finishing notes on her cases for the day. She glanced up at the clock.

She would wait another ten minutes for the American academic. He was late, but the University of Oxford looked favorably on those who brought in their own research grants — and she needed all the help she could get. Morgan pushed her chair back and rolled her shoulders, stretching as she crossed the office to the small kitchen. She refilled her coffee cup, the bitter black her only real addiction.

Her fledgling practice was slowly gaining clients as her expertise at the intersection of religion and psychology became more widely known, but the university still frowned on her specialty. She sometimes wondered what she was trying to prove to herself, let alone others.

Morgan loved working in the ancient city, but the age and status of the university came with drawbacks. It trapped scholars — and all who worshipped at their feet — into well-worn thought patterns with no room for change or progress.

She considered the doors in the Bodleian Library, the venerable institution just around the corner from her office. The names of each School were written above the wooden portals, inscribed in an ancient hand, gold-leafed and stamped into thick oak, banded with copper. Divinity and Scientia were two separate doors, and Morgan sat between them, neither entirely open to her field of research.

Psychology sat within the Faculty of Science, concerned with measurement, the scientific method, and statistical instruments. The Faculty of Theology sat within Divinity, among the monks of Blackfriars, the nuns of the Assumption Convent at Headington, and the Quakers of St Giles.

The Theology curriculum included study of Israel before the exile to Babylon, and St John's Gospel in Greek, while students still debated the Trinity with arguments used by Origen and Augustine, unchanged since the fourth century.

Morgan was an anomaly between the two faculties. Her interest lay in the unexplained between science and faith — that which fell through the gap. Perhaps it was inevitable that her upbringing in Israel had eventually brought her to this place, forever torn between religions, between faith and science, history and the future.

She looked down at the picture of her father on the desk, his smiling eyes captured in the silver frame, and traced his image with a fingertip. He would have been proud of what she had achieved, although he was taken too soon to see it. On the days Morgan felt inadequate, an impostor in this eminent "city of dreaming spires," she remembered he had always believed in her. She carried on for another day in his memory.

Her father's library and study of Kabbalah first inspired Morgan's interest in the psychology of religion, but it had taken years to find her own direction. She joined the Israel Defense Forces, required for all young people, but she stayed on after the mandatory period when they funded her training as a psychologist. She focused on how fundamentalism affected behavior on both sides of the ideological fence, and how the history of the great religions still resonated in the modern world. Evil and violence could be found on all sides and virtue wasn't owned by anyone's god.

Morgan sighed and sat back down, leaning forward to complete her notes as the clock ticked toward ten. The strains of a folk band wafted through her open window from the Turf Tavern just around the corner, the sound of chinking glasses and the hubbub of students a welcome backdrop to her solitary life.

A sharp knock on the door made her jump.

Finally, the academic was here. She could only hope he had an offer worth waiting for.

Morgan walked to the outer office and opened the door.

A man stood outside, clean shaven, dark circles under his eyes emphasized by the shadows of a nearby street lamp. His midnight-blue pinstriped suit was expensive but understated, and he carried a large manila envelope.

"Dr Morgan Sierra?" he asked in an American drawl with hints of the languid South.

"Yes, and you must be Dr Everett?"

He shook his head. "Dr Everett is indisposed. I'm his research assistant, Matthew Fry. I'm so sorry to call this late, but he asked me to come and discuss his proposal. Would you have ten minutes now?"

Fry didn't look like a research assistant, but Morgan knew she didn't look much like the stereotype of an Oxford professor either. With her long dark curls roughly tied back from an angular face, and keen blue eyes with a curious slash of violet in the right, she favored a wardrobe more suited to desert hiking than university meetings.

"Of course, come in." Morgan stepped aside and waved Fry into her spacious office, walled with bookcases.

The books were an eclectic mix of ancient tomes with broken, unrecognizable spines and modern texts, spilling from the shelves to piles on the floor. There was a small reading nook with a cushioned seat surrounded by towering shelves. A skylight high above provided a view of the night sky. A print of a mandala hung on one wall, a circle in a square in hues of turquoise and garnet, one of psychologist Carl Jung's pieces from The Red Book, a private work of religious and occult symbolism recently revealed to the public after years of secret storage. Jung specialized in the psychology of religion and Morgan referenced his work frequently in her own.

Fry opened the manila envelope and spread a series of photos out on her desk. "Thank you for seeing me so late. Dr Everett would like you to work with us on an urgent research project. You're uniquely qualified and we're sure you'll find it challenging — and financially rewarding. We're looking for stones like these."

Morgan walked around the desk and shuffled through the photos. One image caught her eye: a roughly carved stone on a leather cord. She wore a similar one round her neck, hidden under her fitted shirt, a gift from her father not long before he died. It couldn't be a coincidence.

"Why is Dr Everett so interested in these?"

Fry shuffled the images and selected a map of the ancient world dotted with red markers. "Our research shows there are twelve stones spread around the world, precious artifacts from the early Church."

He looked up at Morgan and met her gaze. "We know you have one, and since you're an expert in religious history and psychology, we'd like to employ you to find the rest. We have three stones already, and we need the others as fast as possible."

Morgan shook her head. "Mine has great sentimental value, but that's about it. If it really were some important artifact, it would be in a museum, not with me."

Fry took a step around the desk toward her. "If you won't work with us, we'll buy it. Name your price." He took another step, his face stony. "We know your sister has one, too. The offer includes her stone. We need them both."

Glass smashed in the outer office — the sound of a window breaking.

"Get down," Fry hissed. He flicked back his suit

jacket and pulled a gun from a holster under his arm.

Morgan instinctively ducked down behind her desk, her heart hammering as the thud of two sets of footsteps crunched over broken glass.

The lights went out.

A dim glow filtered through the skylight above, illuminating Fry crouched low to the floor, the gun a flash of silver in his hand. He had clearly come prepared for a fight — but with who?

Morgan cursed under her breath. Back in Israel, her military training kept her alert and ready at all times, but she had lost her edge in this protected pocket of academia. She breathed deeply, trying to slow her heartbeat as memories flooded back.

Israel, under fire in the Golan Heights, her husband Elian by her side, joyous in the adrenalin of battle as he led his team to the front lines. They had both loved defending their country together. But when Elian was killed in a hail of bullets, Morgan left the military behind, the memories too much to bear. Three years had passed since she left the Israeli forces, but her survival skills were still deeply embedded. She could call on them now.

Morgan peered around the edge of the desk. Fry had swiveled the wingback chair to provide cover as he prepared for attack.

But he couldn't hold them off on his own.

This was her terrain. Her responsibility.

Morgan felt around the base of her desk for the compartment fashioned in the wood, a secret place for her gun when she'd dared hope that she would never have to use it again. There were passports too, and wads of cash, just in case. Perhaps she had always known this life was temporary.

The hidden compartment clicked open to reveal her Barak SP-21 pistol. With one breath, it was back in her hand, the familiar weight giving her confidence against the invaders.

Morgan knelt at the edge of the desk, ready to act.

A voice spoke in the darkness with a thick Eastern European accent. "We just want the Apostle's stone. Give it to us and there will be no problems. Dr Sierra, you have a nice, quiet life here. It would be a pity to upset it. All we want is the stone. Toss it toward the door and we'll leave."

Morgan heard both the threat and the promise in his voice. He clearly wasn't with Fry, so who were this other group? She didn't understand why the stone was suddenly so important, but hers alone would not be enough. Her twin sister Faye had one too, and whoever survived this encounter would go after her next.

Fry shuffled into a better position, preparing to fire at the door. "Backup is coming. I'm warning you to leave now."

"Then we'll be quick," the man growled. "You have five seconds to throw the stone out or we're coming in. One…"

Fry turned to Morgan. "You have to get out. Take the stone away from here."

"Two…"

Morgan held her pistol out in front of her with both hands, her eyes on the door as the thumping music from the nearby Turf Pub throbbed with her pulse. "You must know my history, Fry. I can protect myself and, besides, there's no other way out. We have to go through them."

Morgan dashed to the other side of the room, keeping low and out of direct sight of the door, opposite to where Fry crouched behind the chair.

"Three…"

"Don't worry. I've done this before." Morgan's dark smile flashed in the pale light, her lithe body moving with a fluid grace, transformed by the weapon in her hand. No longer an academic, but a soldier once more.

"Four…"

The door burst open.

A rattle of gunfire. Two men in camouflage gear rushed into the room.

Morgan fired and moved position, back behind her desk.

Fry squeezed off two shots, killing one man before being blown back against the oak-paneled wall by the other.

Smoke filled the room.

The smell of sweat and blood took Morgan back to the close-quartered battlefields of Israel's borders. Now it was just her and one attacker remaining.

As her vision narrowed, she reveled in the heightened sensation. It had been too long since she surrendered to the rush. Even now, Morgan resisted the pull of the dark thrill — but this wasn't a fight she could run from.

She peeked around the corner of the desk. The attacker hid behind the bookshelf protruding from the wall in her reading alcove. The little nook was a haven of learning, now polluted by the cold intent of a killer.

His voice came from the shadows. "It's just you and me now. Toss the stone over and I'll leave. Otherwise, I promise you a slow and painful death before I take it anyway — and then I'll visit your sister."

His threatening words brought back memories long buried of torture in a faraway prison. But Morgan didn't break then. This man would not break her now.

The bookcase was a thin veneer, and she knew where each book sat. She could visualize their covers and which ones were tall and short on the shelves. There was a tiny gap where a shot could pass clean through — but once she stood to take it, she would be a clear target.

In one movement, Morgan stood and fired through the bookcase.

The first shot caught the man's ear and knocked him off guard. The framed mandala print smashed down behind him, splintering glass on the floor.

He returned fire, but Morgan moved again, ducking and rolling across the carpet to a better position.

She fired again.

The second shot found its mark in the man's forehead, and he crashed to the floor.

Morgan stood and walked over to the fallen body of her assailant, her heart pounding with the adrenalin of battle. She flicked on the lights, holding her gun on him, just in case. Blood spattered her books and the mandala print. Brain matter dripped down the bookcase onto the carpet.

The man was definitely dead.

She dropped to one knee and frisked his body for identification.

Nothing, except a tattoo on his left forearm, a

stylized horse's head, mouth open with frenzied braying. It was ashen, as if the man's skin had been leached of pigment to make it a paler shade. Morgan took a picture with her phone. Tattoos had a way of betraying the allegiances of their owners and it was all she had to go on for now. The body of the other assailant offered no further clues.

She turned to Fry, his body resting against the wall behind the chair. Morgan closed his eyes out of respect, but she hardly knew the man. She didn't know who this Everett could be either, but clearly there was another group who wanted the stones that she and others held.

There were three bodies in her office, but she couldn't wait for the police. She had to get to Faye. Morgan would protect her sister and her family, and they would run and hide — or fight — if they needed to.

Her quiet academic life was over for now.

She dialed her sister, getting an engaged tone on the landline and no answer on the mobile. "Damn it, Faye, pick up."

Morgan grabbed the rest of her gear from the compartment under the desk, along with more ammunition, and left the building. The music still pumped from the Turf Pub as she emerged onto Holywell Street.

A black van screeched to a halt beside her.

Three men leapt out and pulled her inside, slamming Morgan to the floor and driving off at speed.

CHAPTER 2

THREE MEN HELD MORGAN down, her face pressed hard against the gritty floor of the van. She didn't struggle. There was no use. Better to lie still, listen, and wait for an opportunity.

Her gun was still in her pocket and dug into her thigh. It would only take a second to draw it. She tensed, waiting for the ease of pressure that would surely come. They hadn't killed her, so they couldn't be the same group as the men from her office. Maybe they were Fry's backup team? What the hell was going on?

The van came to a stop, and the pressure lessened.

"Morgan, I'm Jake Timber — a friend." His voice was quiet but authoritative, with a faint South African accent in his deep tone. "Sorry for the rather brusque introduction, but we had to get you off the street. We need to talk. I'm going to let you up now."

As the men relaxed their hold, Morgan curled and sprang up to a kneeling position, gun in hand pointing straight into the face of the man calling himself Jake.

He was dark-haired with a rash of stubble; his amber-brown eyes showed little emotion but his mouth smiled in welcome. Her gun was inches from his nose, but he didn't flinch. A faint scar twisted up, like a mini corkscrew, from his left eyebrow to his hairline. His men hovered just behind her, but he wouldn't have a chance if they tried anything.

Jake held his hands up in surrender. "We need to talk about your stone — and your sister's. Give me ten minutes and then you can leave if you want. We'll send a clean-up crew for the bodies in your office as a peace offering."

Morgan stayed silent, but his words piqued her interest.

He continued, "I'm going to show you something, so you know I'm telling the truth. Can I open my collar?"

She nodded, the weapon unwavering in her hands.

Keeping one hand raised, Jake slowly peeled back the collar of his shirt, revealing a tan leather string. He pulled it up to reveal a stone — not exactly the same as hers, but similar enough.

Fry had not finished his explanation of the stones, let alone why her family was involved, and Morgan needed to know more.

She lowered the gun. "Okay, let's talk, but I want my sister protected, and I want answers *now*."

Jake nodded. "You'll have them soon. Let's go."

After a short drive, Jake opened the van door at a trade entrance at the back of a vast stone building. "It's the Pitt Rivers, next to the Museum of Natural History. Come, I'll explain everything."

Morgan clambered out after him and Jake led the way through the main gallery of the museum, founded in the nineteenth century for the collection of explorer General Pitt Rivers. She had visited the museum by day and found it curious but unthreatening, but in the semi-darkness, the place was alive with menace.

Ritual objects crowded the museum, collected from tribes back in the days of marauding Empire. The deities of different cultures were stuffed into tiny rooms, separated only by the glass of the cabinets, and Morgan could almost imagine them stepping down from their cases in the dark of night to wage war upon each other. The Indian goddess Kali, skulls dripping from her neck and blue skin gleaming, wielded a sword at the head of a tribal god from Benin, as Incan priest icons menaced the Native American totems.

The agony of a Christian martyr twisted toward his God, desperate for release, next to a case of ceremonial knives for stripping the flesh from human sacrifices. A macabre toy cabinet, full of stuffed creatures with beady eyes that seemed to follow the group as they passed. The ghosts of dead children hung in their wake, puppets on tall sticks with broken limbs like dead trees.

Jake led Morgan to the back of the main exhibition hall and down a flight of stairs into the crypt. "Officially, Augustus Pitt Rivers was an eccentric explorer who roamed the British empire, collecting artifacts from now-lost civilizations. But he also worked for a secret government agency on behalf of Queen Victoria. Many of the artifacts you see in the museum are fakes. The genuine items are down here, some a source of ancient power under investigation. Perhaps you know the public face of the agency as the ARKANE Institute?"

Morgan couldn't contain her surprise, her eyes widening at the name. "I've been to some ARKANE conferences. But I thought it was just an academic collective for research and publication."

Jake smiled as they reached a large wooden door at the end of the hall. "That's just the official version. Welcome to the other side of ARKANE."

A small balcony overlooked five levels below, with large glass windows opening to the light well.

Each level had workstations with different artifacts spotlighted upon them, and equipment for dating and analysis. It was empty now, but during the day it was clearly a lab working to fathom ancient secrets.

"I knew there were levels below Oxford," Morgan said. "I've been in the stacks under the Bodleian Library. But how have you kept this all secret?"

Jake raked his hands through his dark hair, exhaustion clear in his eyes.

"There are chambers under Oxford carved out by medieval monks where they taught secrets banned by the university. Occult knowledge needs its protectors and ARKANE is just one in a long line. Few know these secrets, but now you must learn some of them." Jake pointed at the stone. "That puts you and your family in danger."

Morgan touched the worn leather around her neck. "If those men are coming for the stones, you must protect my sister. We each have one."

Jake nodded. "Of course. A team is on the way to her house now, so she and her family will soon be safe, but we need to talk. Come down to the research center and I'll tell you what we know about the stones — and why we have so little time to figure out where they are."

Morgan followed Jake down into a sparsely furnished room with high-tech equipment and a flat, wall-sized computer screen. He tapped at a laptop and brought up an image of the rough-hewn stone that hung around his neck.

He leaned against the wall beside the screen, his athletic body relaxed but alert, muscles taut in tanned forearms under his rolled-up shirt sleeves. He gave the impression of a powerful jungle cat, his dark amber-flecked eyes adding to the illusion.

"The story of the stones is tightly bound into the history of the early Church. Some is history. Some is myth."

Morgan smiled. "And the truth lies somewhere in between, I suppose?"

"Yes, whatever you call truth, that is. Let me tell you what we know."

Jake clicked to a map of Israel. "The story goes back to the Resurrection. After the crucifixion, Matthew's gospel tells of an earthquake that opened the door of the tomb, and the Apostles realized Jesus had risen from the dead."

The image shifted to an open cave door in a garden as Jake continued. "The myth of the stones says that the Apostles took some of the broken rock from the tomb of the risen Christ. They broke it into pieces and used it as the lots cast for the twelfth Apostle, Matthias, then carved the pieces of rock into amulets to wear around their necks as a symbol of their brotherhood."

Morgan touched the stone around her neck. Could it possibly have such a history? "There's no extant tradition I know of this myth, but I guess it's possible. Whatever the truth of their heritage, the symbolism of stone is pervasive in Christian tradition. Like Peter, the rock upon which they built the Church."

The image on the screen changed to a fiery tornado, an image of whirling wind and flame.

Jake continued, "The power of the stones supposedly comes from Pentecost, when the spirit of God gave the Apostles the powers of healing and speaking in multiple tongues, and the ability to convert many to their cause. It's said that the force of wind and fire, combined with the power of Christ's resurrection, became embedded in the stones, causing the miracles that followed the Apostles. When the disciples died or were martyred, the stones were handed down through a network of Keepers."

"So why aren't these stones more well known?" Morgan asked.

Jake clicked through to a map of the ancient world. "When the twelve left Jerusalem, they never met again. They took the gospel to the nations and died at the far corners of the known world. The stones were kept secret, protected as holy artifacts, known only to a few Keepers in each lifetime.

Which brings us to the problem of where they are today."

Dots of various different colors appeared on the map, scattered across the Middle East, North Africa, India, and Europe. "These pins represent the possible journeys of the Apostles after Pentecost — and where the stones may have ended up after they died." He touched the stone around his neck. "This one is supposedly from Matthew Levi, given to ARKANE by the Keeper in Athens before the Second World War in case the Nazis found it."

Morgan frowned. The story seemed so far-fetched, and yet she knew how powerful religious artifacts could seem to those who truly believed.

"So why the sudden interest in the stones now? Why were those men in my office tonight?"

Jake clicked through to an image of Earth, with a circling comet in a wide, elliptical orbit. "This is the Resurgam comet, calculated to return to the atmosphere in the next two weeks, triggering a series of stratospheric events. Scientists predict it will cause extreme weather patterns in many parts of the world. Resurgam is Latin for resurrection. The comet was last in orbit in 33 AD."

Morgan raised an eyebrow. "When Jesus rose from the dead — and perhaps when the stones were empowered at Pentecost?"

Jake nodded. "Exactly. The comet and its associated myth explain the sudden interest in the stones. Thanatos, an extremist religious group, intends to use them to invoke the power of Pentecost. Perhaps to trigger a fundamentalist uprising. Perhaps to start a holy war. And we know of others who seek them, too."

Morgan shook her head. "This is ridiculous. The stones are just pieces of rock, even if they are two thousand years old. They can't have any special power."

"You might be wrong about that." Jake turned, and the screen shifted once more to display an article from the *Times of India* dated only a few weeks before. A pillar of flame leapt out with a headline proclaiming miracles amid a fiery storm.

Morgan scanned the article quickly. "Varanasi… that could be the stone of Nathaniel."

Jake nodded. "ARKANE researchers agree with you. The Apostle Nathaniel, also known as Bartholomew, supposedly died in India after taking the gospel there. A nun disappeared on the night of the miracles, presumed murdered. We believe she was a Keeper." He indicated her stone. "How did you acquire yours?"

Morgan pulled it from her shirt and rubbed her fingers over the rough surface. "My parents were archaeologists, passionate about their work. They met on a dig in Turkey and fell in love amongst the ruins of Ephesus. They found two stones in a commoner's grave and considered them of little value, so they kept them. Faye and I were conceived there, so the twin stones had an emotional resonance."

"What happened to your parents?"

Morgan hesitated. The truth of what happened long ago was a story repeated in so many broken marriages, yet the ripples still affected her life today.

"They couldn't hold their relationship together away from the dig. My father hated the British weather and my mother wanted to live in a more peaceful country, so they separated. My father took me to Israel and Faye stayed here. We were never a family. By the time I came back to England after he was killed in a suicide bombing, my mother had already succumbed to breast cancer."

"I'm sorry," Jake said. "It's tough to lose both parents. Family is everything."

In the silence that followed, Morgan met Jake's unguarded gaze and saw something of her own suffering reflected in his expression. It made her wonder what dark past haunted Jake's nightmares.

His phone rang.

Jake answered and a shadow passed over his face. He clicked on the keyboard and the screen changed to a view from a security camera outside her sister's house. But instead of the quiet scene of the sleepy village, there were flashes of gunfire as the ARKANE team battled with whoever was after the stones.

"Man down, man down. We're under attack. Calling for backup, all units."

Morgan's heart hammered against her ribs as a flush of panic washed over her. She should have gone straight to her family, not spent precious time indulging her curiosity.

A man in black camouflage gear ran out of the back door with Faye slung over his shoulder. Behind him, another man carried a small bundle — her niece, Gemma.

Morgan could only watch in horror. She was too far away to help.

They had taken her family.

CHAPTER 3

Woodstock. Near Oxford, England. May 18

IT TOOK TWENTY MINUTES to reach the house and even though Jake certainly broke the speed limit, Morgan spent every moment wishing she could wind back the clock.

Police circled the perimeter but waved them through once Jake showed his identification to the officer in charge.

Morgan ran into the house ahead of him, needing to be alone. This was her sister's haven, a peaceful retreat from busy city life that Faye cultivated out here in Woodstock. It was far enough away that the little family could keep chickens and stride through the flower meadows together, but it was still close enough to have coffee in central Oxford when the sisters had time to catch up.

The hallway still smelled faintly of fresh bread

Faye must have baked earlier, but it was overlaid by the metallic stench of gunfire. A smell Morgan associated with her time in the military in Israel, not here in quiet, sleepy Oxfordshire.

Faye's husband, David, sat on the sofa in the lounge, surrounded by scattered toys and upended furniture. He stared into a mug of tea as a medic examined him, a blanket over his wide shoulders.

Morgan knelt in front of him. "I'm going to get them back. I promise."

David looked at her with glazed eyes, shock rendering him barely capable of speech. He hunched over his Best Dad In The World mug, his fingers stroking the baby Gemma handprints on the side. "They're everything to me. Who would want to kidnap them? We don't have any money."

Morgan reached out to touch his arm, then pulled back. Her guilt over what had almost happened between them made her even more determined to figure this out. She'd made a promise that night never to hurt her sister, only to keep her safe — and she would keep that vow.

Jake beckoned from the doorway, and Morgan followed him into the kitchen.

"It's unlikely they're dead — for now, at least. Whoever this is will clearly use your sister as a bargaining chip for your stone, and perhaps ours as well."

Morgan sat down at the kitchen table, head in her hands, suddenly overwhelmed. The situation was spiraling out of her control. She should have been here, and Jake had stopped her.

She looked up at him. "I'll happily trade my stone for the lives of my family. You don't even need to be involved."

Jake sat down opposite her at the table. "This is bigger than you and Faye. You saw the paper from India. The stones are potentially powerful. We can't allow them to be gathered together, especially with the Resurgam comet approaching."

Morgan shook her head. "Fanatics always use such events as fuel for their conspiracies. Varanasi could have been mass hysteria, you know that."

Jake took a deep breath and exhaled. "But what if it wasn't? What if the stories of power and the comet event are true? Imagine the force of the stones amplified in a digital age. Such miracles could be enough to spark a new crusade or a holy war. ARKANE exists to shield the world from such events. We keep secrets that the world isn't ready to know yet. We can protect you, and we can find Faye and Gemma. Just give us some time."

Morgan pushed her chair back and stood up. "So much for your all-powerful organization. You couldn't even protect one woman and a child in an Oxford village. I'm doing this alone."

She strode out of the kitchen and ran upstairs to Faye and David's room to gather her thoughts.

The bed was neatly made with a lilac duvet and a crocheted blanket on top, one of her sister's many craft hobbies. Faye's side of the bed had a thick romance novel on the cabinet, next to a well-thumbed Bible and a pot of economy face cream.

Morgan went to the antique dressing table and felt around the back of the pine-framed oval mirror. This had been their agreed-upon hiding place if anything bad happened. Faye laughed when Morgan suggested it over a year ago, insisting there was no need for such a thing. England wasn't Israel, and Morgan was just paranoid.

Now they needed it, but there were no messages. Faye had not known what was coming.

Morgan picked up a photo of the two of them from the dressing table, laughing on a clifftop walk as the wind tangled their hair together. Their faces were similar in bone structure, but apart from that, the twins were light and dark opposites. Morgan had inherited their father's Sephardic Jewish looks, the ebony curls and dusky skin of his Spanish descent. Faye had a Celtic look from their Welsh mother, blonde and fair, with a sprinkling of freckles she tried unsuccessfully to hide. Only their eyes gave their kinship away. Both were blue with an unusual violet slash through them, Morgan's in the right eye and Faye's in the left.

Their parents' personalities were equally represented in the twins; her own passionate, explosive nature and Faye's cool demeanor were diametrically opposed. Their parents couldn't overcome these differences, but perhaps the sisters could succeed where they had failed.

Morgan traced Faye's cheek on the picture with a fingertip, willing strength to her sister, who had helped her start again after Elian's death. There were memories of him everywhere she walked in Jerusalem, but here in the verdant green of England, his ghost remained silent. Faye helped her sister reinvent herself as an academic, and an auntie. Morgan would give everything to bring Faye and Gemma home again — but it was more than just love. Guilt came flooding back as she looked at the wedding photo of a radiant Faye next to her new husband.

That night with David had been an alcohol-induced flirtation, pure and simple.

Morgan had only recently moved to Oxford, and Faye was away for a weekend before the baby was born. The sisters had not yet found a rhythm in their relationship. They still circled each other, questions unasked and shared history buried beneath their parents' skewed remembrances. If she was honest with herself, Morgan knew it was partly jealousy that drove her that night. She wanted Faye's domestic bliss, a haven of peace compared to her own life of upheaval.

Morgan was in a new city. She had lost Elian, her home in Jerusalem — and her father. She was lonely, desperate for a friend and a loving touch.

David called into her office that Friday evening to see if she wanted to have dinner. They went to Browns for mussels and ended up drinking a couple of bottles of wine. They debated religion and psychology, Jung, Freud, and the Bible. Morgan could often out-quote David, even though he was supposedly the learned Christian pastor. They laughed a lot, and it was the most fun she'd had in a long time.

He walked her home to her Jericho flat and came inside for another drink. As she reached for wine glasses in the kitchen, he kissed the back of her neck.

In that moment, Morgan wanted him. Thoughts of Faye were furthest from her mind. She spun in his embrace and, in his kiss, Morgan teetered on the precipice of what could be.

Faye would never know. It would only be one night.

But then she glanced up at the mantelpiece, at a picture of the three of them at the Mansfield College summer party, holding flutes of champagne. As she looked at the sun reflecting off their laughing faces, Morgan realized how close she was to losing everything.

She pushed David away.

They both wanted more, but they knew this could never happen again. Faye was his wife and her twin. He was a pastor. What they contemplated was a sin, even if you didn't believe in God.

The two of them never mentioned it again and maintained a certain professional distance.

Since then, she and Faye had finally found the relationship that twins were supposed to have. They finished each other's sentences and picked up the phone just as the other called. Morgan was Gemma's devoted auntie, who the little girl called for when she was sick, who brought her surprise presents. They were her family, and Faye and Gemma were all that mattered now.

Morgan sighed and walked into Gemma's room, a kaleidoscope of rainbow colors, books, and stuffed toys. Her favorite teddy lay discarded on the floor.

As tears welled, Morgan picked it up and hugged it to her. "I'm coming, Gemma."

Feeling eyes on her back, she spun to see Jake in the doorway.

"Come downstairs," he said. "We've found a package — and it's addressed to you."

Morgan followed Jake back downstairs to the living room, where he indicated a parcel on the table, wrapped in thick brown paper tied up with string.

"We've scanned it for explosives. It's safe."

Morgan carefully untied the string and pulled apart the paper. It contained two black Moleskine notebooks and a phone.

They waited while a police officer processed the items for prints, then Morgan picked up the phone. It was unlocked, with a video file ready on the home screen.

She clicked play.

A close-up of a flickering fire. The crackle of flame.

A voice spoke with an American accent that grated over them. "Apologies for the intrusion, Morgan, but taking your sister and the little one was necessary. Time is running out. The myth of the stones will become a reality on the day of Pentecost when the comet reaches its zenith and I call down the power of miracles. As it was two thousand years ago, so it shall be again. I'm inviting you as my guest to the event. Of course, you'll need to bring the other stones, otherwise your sister and niece will become a fiery sacrifice, just like the Keeper from Varanasi."

The video zoomed through the flames to show a burned body, skin crackling, bones splitting, mouth open in a final agonized scream.

David turned away, retching.

The voiceover continued. "I need all twelve stones for the day of Pentecost. Bring the rest to me, Morgan, if you want your family back. Your refusal to join me has forced my hand, and another party also pursues the stones."

The screen changed to display the image of a pale horse's head. Morgan recognized the tattoo from the attacker's arm, but only now did its significance become clear.

"Before me was a pale horse," she whispered. "Its rider was named Death and Hell followed close behind him. From Revelation chapter six."

The voice continued. "This shadowy group calls themselves Thanatos. They collect occult and religious objects of power and they will stop at nothing to get the stones of the Apostles. Stay ahead of them if you want your family back. I used my father's biblical research to find three stones, but time is short. I need someone with more knowledge and more… motivation to find the rest by Pentecost Sunday, May 27th, in nine days' time. Keep the phone on and I'll contact you with a location. If you don't deliver, I'll continue my experiments with fire on human flesh."

As the video ended, Morgan took a breath and slowly exhaled. At least now she had a direction to go in. Faye and Gemma were the priority, but she also felt the first tendrils of intrigue at the possibilities of the stones.

She looked over at Jake. "That's Everett, the American academic. ARKANE must be able to trace his whereabouts."

Jake nodded, pulling out his phone. "On it."

David gripped the edge of the table, knuckles white, his face pale. "Do what that man said, Morgan. You can't risk their lives. Please, bring them home."

"Of course. I'll do whatever it takes. We'll find them."

David turned and walked from the room, his shoulders hunched, his stature diminished by the weight of fear.

Morgan picked up one of the Moleskine journals and flicked through the first few pages. There were notes and diagrams in spidery handwriting and a map of Europe and the Near East with red dots and lines drawn on it.

Jake stood next to her and bent to examine it

more closely. "It's similar to the ARKANE map of where the Apostles traveled. You need resources and backup if you want to find the other stones in time. We have contacts all over the world, facilities, and transport. We can support you with whatever you need."

As much as she wanted to refuse his offer outright, Morgan knew it would be impossible to find the stones alone — and on her limited budget. Jake offered a lifeline, but she was wary of him.

"I'll think about it. Did you find out which Apostles our stones belonged to? I need to narrow down the places to look for the others."

"Our research suggests that you have the stone of the Apostle John, the author of Revelation, and Faye has the stone of James Alphaeus."

"How come ARKANE had one stone all this time but didn't collect the rest?"

Jake grinned, his corkscrew scar spiraling up to his brow. "Do you know how many Christian relics and artifacts there are in the world?"

Morgan couldn't help but laugh, despite the dire situation. "Enough of the true cross to fill a forest and enough holy nails to build a city. I see what you mean."

"Exactly. It was just another unsubstantiated myth before the miracles of Varanasi and the discovery of the Resurgam comet."

"And until my sister and niece were kidnapped."

Jake nodded. "Of course. But you have to let us help. There's no way you can find the other stones alone in nine days."

Morgan hesitated. She was used to doing things her way, but she couldn't let pride or stubbornness stop her from rescuing her family.

She nodded. "Okay, we'll work together for now and come to some agreement about the stones later. At least it buys us some time."

Jake reached out a hand. "I know it's not ideal, but with your religious knowledge and ARKANE resources, we'll find the stones and get your family back. Our team will work overnight digitizing and cross-checking the diaries and we'll get started tomorrow."

After a slight hesitation, Morgan shook his hand and nodded her assent. She would go along with this partnership for now, but she had every intention of exchanging the stones for her family. If Jake stood in her way, she would go around him — or through him.

As soon as Morgan left the Woodstock house, Jake went outside and called the ARKANE Director, Elias Marietti, on a secure line.

"I've convinced her she needs us. I won't be able to get her stone right away, but I think she can lead us to the others… You were right about Thanatos being after them… Yes, the sister will give hers up, too. I'll make sure of it."

He hung up and looked back through the windows of the house. David sat upstairs with his head in his hands, shoulders heaving. It must be the little girl's bedroom.

Jake turned away. This wasn't the time to be sentimental. The mission would always take precedence, and collateral damage was inevitable.

CHAPTER 4

Tucson, Arizona, USA. May 19

Joseph Everett walked into St Bartholomew's private psychiatric unit, where his twin brother, Michael, had lived for the past fifteen years.

The hospital was a pleasant, sterile facade laid over a maelstrom of human misery. Colorful wall paintings camouflaged the suffering behind every door, with drugs and behavior modification necessary to maintain a superficial calm. But it was the best hospital in Arizona, and Joseph had no choice but to keep Michael here and visit as often as he could.

The warden at the front desk acknowledged his passing with a nod. Joseph left his keys and other sharp objects at the security gate and proceeded through the main corridors to the dayroom.

Michael sat in his usual seat by the window, staring out at the garden, legs hugged to his chest.

He never looked at his brother, never seemed to hear any words spoken to him, yet Michael was placid and would take his meds, lie down when told, and sleep. He was merely empty, a shell of a man.

Joseph smoothed the hair back from his brother's forehead, but, as ever, there was no response.

They were twins of a sickly opposite. Both were lean, but Joseph's muscles were well defined and he walked tall and strong. Michael was wasted and weak, with cheekbones that almost protruded through his pale skin and lips tinged with blue. Joseph spoke with vigor and moved with grace, while his brother was silent and gaunt, folded into immobility.

Joseph turned to the nurse on duty. "How is he today?"

They went through this ritual every time, and her reply was usually the same. But today she started at his approach. "I need to get the doctor to speak with you."

She left the room and returned with Dr Campbell, his expression serious, a thick folder clutched in one hand. He indicated a private room where they could talk.

"We need to discuss how best to manage the next steps for Michael. He's been wasting away for months now, and he's too thin and sick for the main facility. We need to move him to the hospice ward."

Joseph shook his head emphatically. "No. He's fine here. He's going to get better, I know it."

Dr Campbell opened the thick file and pointed at the latest test results. "It's all here. I'm sorry, Joseph. I know what Michael means to you, but you have to face facts. We can make him comfortable, but he's reached a threshold."

Joseph took a step closer to the doctor, his lips thin, his body taut with barely restrained anger. "How dare you? I've given the hospital millions in donations. There must be more you can do."

The doctor shook his head. "I'm sorry. The end is coming. You've been the most devoted of brothers, but you can't do anything else now except help him die with dignity. I'll leave you to think about it."

Dr Campbell left the room. Joseph stood motionless while his world collapsed around him. He gazed down at the patterns on the carpet, the inoffensive grey and pink swirls designed to mute the sounds of suffering this room witnessed every day. He pushed his fists against his temples, knuckles white.

There was still a chance, but he couldn't tell the doctor of his plan.

Pentecost was only days away and, with the miracles of the stones, he might still save his brother from a wasting death. There had been healings in the wake of Varanasi — he just needed to know how to harness and direct the power.

Returning to the day room, Joseph pulled up a chair next to Michael, held his hand, and talked quietly, as was their regular ritual.

Sometimes he reminisced about their childhood, but mostly he spoke of what was on his mind, another day in the life of a wealthy business executive, politician, and pillar of the community in Tucson, Arizona. Immigration issues, the vagaries of the housing market, and protests outside his office about water shortages in the desert region. He had posed as an academic to get close to Morgan Sierra, but academia was far from his real life.

Michael had become a diary of sorts, a soul into which he poured his heart so that when he left, Joseph felt lighter and rejuvenated. It didn't matter that his words merely washed over his brother, who never spoke or even looked at him. Joseph was sure he listened and understood.

He gently stroked his brother's thin hair, his determination solidifying. Michael deserved the gift of healing after everything they had been through.

The twins had been late additions to a miserable marriage and the target of their mother's fury with the world. Their father had been mostly absent, consumed with biblical research. He cared nothing for raising children and shut himself away in his study when he was home. He often traveled, bringing back strange objects he kept locked away from their prying eyes and sticky fingers.

The twins were hardly seen and definitely not heard; their mother made sure of that. She was the one who roamed their nightmares. She made them wash all the time, calling them dirty and filthy, scrubbing them with pumice stones until their young skin was raw and bleeding. They were stains she wanted to erase from her crumbling world.

Michael was the older twin by minutes and played the protector, deflecting their mother's attention. She beat him with sharp metal kitchen tools, then shut them both under the stairs in the dark. Michael would hold his brother until Joseph's terrified sobbing slowed and they slept curled up, arms around each other.

They were safe together.

After growth spurts in their teens, Joseph became more resilient and able to fend for himself. At thirteen, Michael stopped speaking, communicating only with his hands or writing on scraps of paper. Joseph understood his brother's sign language, but their mother couldn't bear the control he claimed over his own body. In a rage, she forced Michael's hand onto the burner of the stove to make him scream. He hadn't made a sound, and she only stopped when the stench of burning flesh brought Joseph running to help.

At fifteen, Michael tried to cut off his penis with a knife in front of their mother. She laughed and urged him on. Joseph wrested the knife away from his brother, but the cut was deep.

Joseph called 911 and told them everything.

After social services removed the twins, Michael entered his first psychiatric ward, and never left. While his twin's condition grew worse every year, Joseph emerged as an up-and-coming business executive. As he made more money, he moved Michael into better facilities, and always lived close to the hospital so he could visit regularly. But despite his success, Joseph still felt he was trapped in that closet with his brother.

He needed Michael — and he would do whatever he could to save his twin.

Joseph leaned in close so the nurses couldn't overhear. "I'm going to take you on a trip soon. I've found a way to help you, but I just need a little more time. Don't worry, it won't be long now and then we'll be together."

Private airstrip, Surrey, England. May 19.

Faye woke as early morning light filtered through a tiny window and seeped under the doorframe. She raised her head tentatively — but explosive pain left her gasping. A gag covered her mouth, so she breathed in and out slowly through her nose until the nausea passed.

Where was Gemma? Was she okay?

Looking around frantically, Faye saw her daughter curled up near the foot of the chair. While her attackers had bound Faye's arms and legs, Gemma was free to move. They knew she wouldn't leave her mother once she revived from the drugs. The little girl's face was pale and creased, but she breathed normally and didn't seem to be injured.

Faye desperately wanted to take Gemma in her arms, hold her close — but she couldn't move.

She took a mental inventory of her body, checking for injury and pain. She was bruised, but more or less uninjured.

Faye thought back to the night before. She had been listening to a talk show and didn't hear them come in. A man grabbed her from behind and pushed her to the floor, jabbing a needle into her neck. The world faded to black. No time to even scream.

She prayed David was okay, that they hadn't hurt him. He would have fought for his family, and she could only hope he hadn't resisted too hard. At least she and Gemma were alive, but what could they possibly have that was worth kidnapping for?

Faye prayed silently. God would protect them through whatever trials they faced, but they needed to escape from here somehow.

She was restrained in a large storage closet with high ceilings and a tiny window too far up to reach. The walls were metal, lined with shelves stacked with all kinds of tools. Potential weapons — if only she could get to them.

Gemma whimpered. Her eyes fluttered open, and she looked around groggily, then faded back into sleep. Faye was grateful that her baby was unaware of her surroundings. Perhaps this would just be a bad dream, one that would be over soon because it had to be a mistake.

She heard the roar of a plane taking off outside. They must be at an airport. If they were taken out of the country, how would anyone find them?

Faye frantically pulled at the ties holding her hands and feet, wriggling in an attempt to get them loose. Raw skin bled at her wrists. Tears pricked her eyes. Her frustration rose as she realized the bonds were too tight.

The door slammed open. A stocky man stood in the doorway, a cup of steaming coffee in his hand, the smell wafting toward her. He was unshaven, his eyes baggy from a night without sleep.

Faye could see past him into a hangar where several small planes were parked. Two other men stood looking with interest in her direction, making no attempt to hide their identities. She looked away, refusing to acknowledge them.

The man walked over, chuckling. "You won't ignore me for long."

He stroked her cheek, his voice low, as he placed his coffee on a box. He cupped her chin, making her face him, and with his other hand, he squeezed her breast hard. Faye winced, tears welling in her eyes.

"Be a good girl, or your daughter is next."

He laughed and let her go, swinging his leg back as if to kick the little bundle of Gemma at her feet.

Faye lunged forward in the chair to protect her child from this monster.

But she only toppled sideways onto the floor, smacking her head on the concrete. The man laughed, and she heard the amusement of the other men outside, a camaraderie of humiliation.

As he bent down to pull her upright, the man's phone rang.

He left Faye and answered it, pulling the door almost shut behind him.

She could still hear his words through the crack.

"Yeah, they're okay. The plane is due to take off in two hours. We'll be with you tomorrow, boss. No problems this end."

Faye realized then that there was no mistake; somehow they were the target of a kidnapping.

Her thoughts went to Morgan, the sister who kept so much hidden from her past. David would only know to call the police and leave it to them, but she knew Morgan would act. She was a wild creature that Oxford tried in vain to groom into a domestic academic, but Morgan would never fit into that box. Faye knew her sister would do anything for Gemma; the little girl represented a hope that their family could start again, and build a new life around the future instead of the past.

Faye shifted on the ground as her back arched into painful spasms. Gemma stirred and opened her eyes, still sleepy, on the edge of consciousness. Faye smiled and made soft, loving noises to calm her. The little girl crawled closer and cuddled into her mother.

They were both alive and that was enough for now. Faye prayed into the beginning of a new day — for the strength to protect her daughter, and for the sister she knew would come for them.

CHAPTER 5

ARKANE Headquarters. London, England. May 19

JAKE TIMBER WALKED THE short distance from Embankment tube station to ARKANE's hidden entrance, a nondescript doorway on Duncannon Street next to the Halfway to Heaven pub, an appropriate name given what lay beneath.

Most visitors approached the official entrance of the ARKANE Institute at the corner of the Strand and St Martin's Place, where several floors of offices graced the top levels of the building. Windows looked out over Trafalgar Square, flanked by Corinthian columns with a balcony topped by a flagpole, the Union Jack flying proudly in the breeze. But the public face of ARKANE was a smokescreen for its true purpose.

Started as a purely Christian defense in England, the Arcane Religious Knowledge And Numinous Experience — or ARKANE — Institute developed over the years into an organization investigating supernatural and religious mysteries around the world. Its official wing ran publications and seminars with experts speaking at all the right conferences, but only a few in the top echelons of government knew about its secret side.

The authorities called ARKANE when events spiraled beyond the physical realm, when the police or other agencies needed experts in this unusual field. A secret Act of Parliament circumscribed their remit and ARKANE worked above the law of the lands they operated in, hidden in the shadows investigating that which no one would admit to.

In a modern world where ancient faith played an increasingly political role, they were often behind the scenes at the crux of international flash-points. Their elite teams pursued the evil that humans conjure and use against one another even as it stalks their souls. They collected artifacts and manuscripts of power that could be used as weapons and a host of unseen things that were better off being denied. Strands of truth underpin myths that span millennia — and sometimes the evidence remained hidden in the ARKANE vaults under London.

Jake put his eye to the retinal scanner of the elevator entrance and descended below the throngs of tourists heading to Piccadilly Circus.

The ARKANE headquarters extended beneath the crypt of St-Martin-in-the-Fields church and under Trafalgar Square in the heart of London. Designed by Sir Charles Barry in 1845, the plans of its subterranean structure were kept in hidden archives, protected as secrets of the realm.

A tunnel led straight to No. 10 Downing Street, the residence of the British Prime Minister. In the days when those in office cared about religious and supernatural affairs, they often used it for secret meetings. But the entrance was sealed after the Second World War and now the Prime Minister was mostly in the dark about the occult knowledge that lay hidden so close to the halls of power.

Jake walked along the central corridor toward the main research rooms, his thoughts preoccupied with questions about the stones — and Morgan Sierra. He mostly worked alone or led a small team and he was wary of an unpredictable, if highly capable, outsider.

Glass-paneled doors marked the offices where small teams analyzed artifacts or examined ancient manuscripts. The historic brick structure had been converted into the most technologically advanced research suites in the world, all with high-level security — necessary to protect the secrets within.

There was no natural light in the underground

section, but the lighting was subtly tuned to mimic bright daylight. Intricate trompe l'oeil paintings decorated some walls with windows looking out onto the Mediterranean Sea, the Egyptian pyramids, and a gabled view of the Eiffel Tower, evocative of ARKANE's many international missions.

Jake headed toward Martin Klein's office, one of the tiniest rooms at ARKANE — but its significance belied its size.

Martin was officially head archivist but widely considered to be the brain of the institute. He spent his days writing intricate code linking vast databases of knowledge retrieved through official channels — and through more clandestine means. Martin perceived patterns where others could see nothing and, while he pondered the deeper problems, he created worlds on the walls of his office in colored markers, drawing fantastical creatures and plants in otherworldly scenes of beauty. Every few months, the entire office would be painted white and he would begin again on the fresh canvas.

He was a tall man with a shock of blond hair. He couldn't bear to be touched by a barber, so he roughly chopped it himself with scissors when hunks of it began falling down over his eyes. His glasses had thin wire rims, the lightest he could bear on his sensitive skin.

While Martin's mathematical and data processing ability lay at genius level, he did not understand the subtleties of human interaction. Some would label such a personality, but Martin transcended all such labels with his ability to figure out almost unsolvable problems. He had earned his affectionate nickname, Spooky, many times over — and Jake needed his help now.

Jake knocked on the door of Martin's office and walked inside.

Martin spun around in his desk chair and jumped up, bobbing toward Jake before retreating to his desk. "Welcome back. What do you need?"

There was never any small talk with Martin. He didn't waste time, and given how many open missions ARKANE had at any one time and how many lives could be at stake, Jake was fine with that.

"Have you been able to find anything more about viable locations for the stones?"

Martin sat back down at his desk and tapped out a staccato rhythm on the keyboard, pointing out the data on four monitors arrayed in front of him.

"I've triangulated mentions of the Apostles in the historical record and Christian literature and compiled them with the topography of the regions. It certainly narrows down potential search possibilities."

Martin's custom databases and search engine were unique to ARKANE, designed and programmed as his first job after Director Marietti recruited him from Cambridge with a double doctorate in computer science and archaeology. His ongoing mission was to make sense of the chaos of ever-expanding data. He built specialized character recognition scanners and software, tying ancient texts to multiple translations, linking legends with satellite maps and images, until patterns emerged from the riot of information.

Jake examined these patterns now, seeing how far the Apostles had roamed in their sacred quest. "That's a great start. What about Everett's location?"

"I hacked into his home surveillance system in Arizona, but there's no sign of Dr Sierra's family. He has a complicated setup of shell companies, so I'm cross-checking with land ownership databases in case he's holding them elsewhere. We're monitoring him for now, but Marietti said to let the mission run without intervening at this point."

Jake understood that the Pentecost stones were the primary mission objective, but if they could locate Morgan Sierra's family, she might be more willing to give up her stone without a fight.

"I need to find out some other information. Can I use the pod?"

Martin didn't look up from his screens. "Of course."

Jake walked over to what looked like a tanning booth squashed between Martin's desk and the back wall of the office. It was a prototype user interface for ARKANE's vast store of digital knowledge, a virtual library where users could interact with the information. Martin based it on the Radcliffe Camera of Oxford's Bodleian Library, an old-fashioned skin over a highly technical, relational database.

Jake entered the pod and pulled the door shut behind him. The device initialized, and the open space of the Radcliffe Camera appeared, surrounded by stacks of books and a high ceiling that stretched into the dome above. Even the quality of light was softer here, with rays of sunlight streaming in from arched windows.

The librarian walked out from behind the stacks, an archetype with brunette bun, glasses, and buttoned-up beige cardigan. "What can I help you with?"

"Morgan Sierra, psychologist and lecturer at the University of Oxford. What do you have on her?"

As the librarian accessed the databases, her image flickered a little. Then she smiled and passed Jake a folder that opened up to a full screen in front of him.

He scrolled through the information, flicking through Morgan's history displayed in images, documents, and even audio and video clips. Jake stopped at her record from the Israel Defense Forces. He felt a twinge of guilt at examining her life this way, but he needed to know who he was dealing with.

The IDF had funded Morgan's psychology studies, where she specialized in religious fundamentalism. She directed a team investigating ways to change the hearts and minds of those who hated Israel. There were also videos of her competing in national competitions for Krav Maga, an Israeli martial art that she clearly excelled at.

Her mental health status was variable, especially after the death of her husband, Elian, killed in active service. She had been there when he died.

Her parents were deceased, her father murdered by a suicide bomber on the number twelve bus in downtown Beersheba, Israel. There were shots of body parts strewn amongst metal shards and shopping bags. One picture showed a sack of oranges, their bright color drawing the eye, as a severed arm reached for them in the foreground.

After the death of her father and husband, Morgan left Israel for life as an academic. Jake wondered whether the memories of violence still haunted her, as the death of his own family tormented endless nights. Did it make her an unstable partner?

A ping sounded, and a message from Martin flashed in the corner of the screen.

Marietti wants to see you. NOW.

CHAPTER 6

Blackfriars. Oxford, England. May 19

FATHER BEN COSTANZA KNELT in the dim light of Blackfriars chapel, his head bent in prayer as he counted the maple wood rosary beads tied at his waist, his fingers moving slowly from the arthritis that sapped his dexterity.

The church was simple for a Catholic place of worship, with white stone walls lit by high windows. There was no stained glass, only clear panels surrounded by decorative stonework. Motes of dust floated in the light from the windows, streaming down to the altar of russet-speckled marble. Plain wooden choir stalls stood before it with hard, straight-backed chairs for the congregation. A modest place for a pure faith.

Years of devotion had strengthened Ben's knees, but his joints still protested as he sat back into the pew. He sighed. In his mind, he was still a young man, but time had taken its toll. He had worshipped in this chapel for nearly forty years, his passion for teaching earning him a permanent place at the Dominican College as a tutor for the Angelicum, the baccalaureate in sacred theology, granted by the Pontifical University of St Thomas in Rome.

The Blackfriars — Dominican monks — had established a priory in Oxford in 1221 when the Regent Master of the university joined the Order. It was a working priory until 1538, when Henry VIII dissolved the monasteries, and the monks were scattered. Over four hundred years later, the Blackfriars priory bustled with life on busy St Giles, a main road into the center of Oxford, between the Ashmolean Museum and Little Clarendon Street.

The area was home to the university offices, ice cream parlors, and bars frequented by students living in this end of town. Amongst these modern distractions, Blackfriars continued as a working priory, dedicated to a common life of prayer, study, and teaching. The daily mass was open to the public and a small congregation formed around the community, in addition to the students who came for weekly tutorials. Ben was content here.

He crossed himself and left the chapel. He glanced at his watch and hurried across the quad. Morgan would arrive soon and it sounded like the reason for her visit was more serious than their usual weekly catch-up about gossip in the theological community.

Morgan's specialty meant she was often in the center of the latest storm of controversy. Ben enjoyed hearing about it and found that his age gave him a perspective that few others shared.

The theological contentions they raged over had been debated for millennia, by far better scholars, to no satisfactory conclusion. In God's wisdom, he allowed believers to have diverse views, but faith was of the heart and the head was only ever a distraction. Regardless, Ben still enjoyed the gossip about who was feuding with whom.

His time with Morgan also gave him an insight into a university that was swiftly moving away from old men like him. As she found her way into college life and built her own psychology practice, they met weekly for coffee and surreptitious sticky buns in his tiny office at Blackfriars.

As Ben rounded the corner, he saw Morgan already standing outside his study, her brow furrowed with concern. She looked exhausted, and she rubbed the stone around her neck like a charm.

Ben worried about her like a father. He was acutely aware that he could never replace those she had lost, but given his monastic life, she and her sister were as close as he could get to having a family.

Morgan glanced up and a brief smile flickered over her face. They hugged, and he ushered her inside.

Ben listened as she told him about Faye and Gemma, the stones of the Apostles, and the need to swiftly find the remaining artifacts before Pentecost Sunday, when the comet would be in ascendance.

Morgan paced his office, only managing a few steps in the small space before turning around. "What do you think, Ben? Could the stones have belonged to the Apostles — and even have real power?"

Ben sighed. "The stones are clearly a matter of faith for those who seek them, so it doesn't matter what we think. Faith can indeed move mountains, but it can also destroy lives."

He sat back and pondered his bookshelf, the ancient tomes perhaps containing some wisdom they could use now. One of the Master Generals of the Order had said, 'Divine wisdom is like a spring that comes down from heaven through a pipeline of books.' In Ben's experience, there was always a book that could help.

There were many dangers in Morgan's quest, but he couldn't send her away without trying. He had been a friend of her parents, back when he briefly worked as an archaeologist, before his calling. Ben hadn't agreed with how they'd managed the divorce and split the twins, and there were aspects of those times that continued to haunt his nightmares — but he would always help Morgan and her sister.

Ben reached up for an antique tome and opened it to a map of the ancient world at the time of Christ.

"Little is known of the Apostles after the book of Acts, but death will often point the way. I have some contacts in the Vatican who might help you with locations."

Morgan shook her head. "No need. An organization specializing in religious artifacts, the ARKANE Institute, is helping me. You must have heard of them?"

Ben's heart pounded in his chest at her words. The secrets ARKANE kept hidden were like the demons that crept under the battlement of prayer each night.

Morgan put her hand on his arm. "Are you okay, Ben?"

He leaned forward, his voice husky with concern. "There are things you should know about ARKANE, people you need to be careful of."

She frowned. "But I need their help to find the stones. It's the only way to find Faye and Gemma in time."

Ben walked to the window and stared out at the quad. "Don't trust them, Morgan. I worked with some of their agents once, a long time ago. They have information that can bring down governments and change the world order. There are shadows behind their shining public face."

He turned back to face her. "If ARKANE is interested in these stones, then perhaps the artifacts are more than they seem. There *are* miracles on this earth, some indeed from the divine — but others from the Deceiver."

The sudden smash of breaking glass made him duck.

An object came hurtling through the window behind Ben's head as the sound of gunfire erupted in the quadrangle beneath them.

Morgan saw the grenade as it landed.

Her years of military training kicked in and she yanked Father Ben out of the tiny office into the stone corridor, slamming the door shut just before the grenade exploded inside.

The force knocked them both to the ground. Ben lay coughing and wheezing on the ground. The thick college walls contained most of the blast, but it might have just been a ploy to flush them out.

She grabbed Father Ben's arm and helped him up. "We've got to get out of here."

Smoke poured out of the office as fragments of paper and ash floated on the toxic breeze. Gunfire and screams echoed up the stairwell from the quad below.

Sudden footsteps thudded on stone, coming closer.

Ben pointed to the end of the corridor. "Where the stairwell ends, there is a narrow staircase, but few know of it."

They hurried down the passage. Ben pulled back a tapestry on the wall to reveal a narrow doorway and fumbled at his waist for a key.

"Here we go. Bother, it's sticky. Give me a minute."

"We don't have a minute, Ben. Hurry."

Morgan stood facing the stairwell, listening to the running feet approach. She moved into a Krav Maga fighting stance and slowed her breathing. She would not go easily, even in the face of firepower.

"It's open. Let's go."

Ben's voice broke her concentration. Morgan turned and edged through the tiny doorway after him, pulling the tapestry down and the door almost closed just as footsteps hammered up the stairs. She dared not pull the door completely shut, as the creaking would surely give them away.

They waited motionless, hardly breathing.

Voices outside the door, muffled by the heavy tapestry. "She's not here. There must be another exit. Search the other rooms."

After a pause, the frantic voice of a petrified monk dragged from his hiding place echoed down the hall.

Morgan found Ben's hand in the dark and squeezed it, urging him not to move. She was torn between her need to keep him safe and her need to escape — but she couldn't let this monk suffer for her sake.

"Where are they?"

A fleshy thud made Ben shudder as the monk cried out in pain.

Morgan needed to get the men's attention. She whispered under her breath, "Get ready to run."

Ben stepped back and Morgan pushed the door, sending the tapestry billowing into the corridor and revealing their hiding place.

She pulled it shut again, slamming it hard.

They raced down the two flights to the bottom.

Ben was doing well so far, but Morgan knew he wouldn't be able to keep up once they were out of the building. "Where does this come out?"

"Behind the Ashmolean Museum," Ben panted. "There's a service entry at the back."

"I need you to get inside the museum and stay somewhere public. They're after me, so you should be okay."

They reached the bottom of the stairs as the door at the top blasted open.

Running footsteps.

The sound of a radio and a call for backup.

The invaders would be on their heels soon enough.

In Krav Maga, running away was always preferable to fighting. Sometimes Morgan railed against it, but this was indeed a battle she needed to run from, not try to fight.

She pushed open the last door and pulled Ben out into the bright day, propelling him across the gravel to the back entrance of the Ashmolean. "Go, I'll find you later."

He touched her cheek softly. "Be careful."

Morgan watched him scurry into the museum complex, a haven of academics, tourists and security guards. Ben would be safe there.

Keeping low, Morgan ran around the back of Blackfriars, through the thick trees and into St Cross College, which adjoined it to the north. This was her turf. She knew the labyrinth of college grounds and she would evade the men soon enough.

As she ran, Ben's warning echoed in Morgan's

mind, but time ticked away toward Pentecost and the flames of judgment. She had to get to Faye and Gemma — and ARKANE was her only option.

Father Ben eventually returned to his office, after running the gauntlet of the police and the questions of his superiors in the Order. He had clutched his chest and wheezed vague answers. Age was a convenient excuse indeed.

Ben walked slowly back up the stairs to his study, but as he entered, he clutched the doorframe in horror.

The room had been torn apart, both by the grenade that had shredded most of his precious books — but also by human hands ripping through his belongings.

A rough drawing marked the bookcase: a pale horse's head, drawn in thick black lines and colored chalky white.

A flash of memory and Ben was back in the ancient ruins of Ephesus half a lifetime ago, watching as a man on the edge of insanity sketched this very symbol. A man who must surely be dead, but whose past was entwined with ARKANE and whose heart was black with murder.

"Thanatos," he whispered. "Be careful, Morgan."

CHAPTER 7

ARKANE Headquarters. London, England. May 19

JAKE TOOK THE ELEVATOR from the vaults below up the eight floors to the penthouse of the ARKANE Institute and stood silently in the doorway to the grand office.

Director Elias Marietti stood gazing out the bay window, the grey London light giving his face an ashen pall. Papers were strewn across a large mahogany desk, once the property of George Frederic Watts, a Victorian painter who had seen visions of God but rejected conventional religion. The director had seen the irony in that. One of Watts's paintings hung on the office wall, a loan from the Tate Gallery: *'She shall be called woman'*, a vision of the creation of Eve, with life force blown from above into a figure surrounded by billowing clouds.

Marietti turned and waved Jake in, skipping the

small talk as usual. "The celestial events associated with the Resurgam comet are accelerating. You must not let the Pentecost stones come together at its zenith. I'm concerned about the involvement of Thanatos. I had thought them long gone."

Marietti sighed, and Jake could almost see the weight of responsibility on his shoulders.

They had worked together for years now and he knew the director well. Marietti recruited Jake back when he worked in Africa, overseeing aid in Sudan. His special military team had been ordered to stand by and could only watch as the National Islamic Front slaughtered Catholics, including children. It was a political decision, and there was nothing they could do but wait it out.

The Vatican sent Marietti as a representative of the Holy See during the terrible war that raged senselessly for years. Late one night, Jake stood with him on a verandah in the dark, listening to screams in the distance.

Jake had cursed God for the blood on their hands, but Marietti explained it was not God but humanity who twisted faith toward evil. Religion had torn humanity apart for millennia and it would never stop — but there was a way to be part of the solution.

He'd told Jake of ARKANE, a covert group

investigating spiritual mysteries and supernatural enigmas. Jake joined soon after and the ARKANE missions had given them both purpose over the years — but the challenge never stopped. Evil didn't sleep and the continued missions took their toll.

"What do you know of Thanatos?" Jake asked.

Marietti sat down at the desk, hands folded under his chin. "It was formed after the Second World War, a splinter group searching for powerful occult objects based on Nazi research, using perversions of ancient prophecy to proclaim the end of days. I thought we defeated them back then, but clearly they went underground, only emerging now because of the potential power of the stones."

Marietti passed a photo across his desk. "While Thanatos pursues a religious crusade, Joseph Everett's motivation is more personal. This is his brother Michael, currently dying in an Arizona psychiatric ward. It looks like he wants the stones to heal his brother — and after the miracles of Varanasi, it's certainly possible."

Marietti's dark eyes were black in the dim light, his bushy eyebrows overshadowing a craggy face that had seen so much. He was silent for a moment, then stood again and walked around his desk.

"The stones haven't been in the same place since Pentecost over two millennia ago. Separately, they are powerful artifacts. Together with the comet, they may be catastrophic." Marietti put his hand on Jake's shoulder. "These are dangerous times. Bring the stones back here… at any price."

With Marietti's words echoing in his mind, Jake left the office and walked out onto the Strand, a busy hub of London traffic and tourism.

He merged into the crowd and walked back toward Embankment tube station, his thoughts straying to Morgan Sierra. Her past had clearly left scars, but she would do anything to get her family back — while his loyalties lay only with ARKANE. Conflict was inevitable, but they had to work together for now.

His phone rang.

"Jake, it's Morgan. I was attacked at Blackfriars. I think it was Thanatos. Clearly, they won't stop until they have my stone. We have to stay ahead of them — and I think I know where we need to start."

Brize Norton airfield, England. May 20.

As they sat in the Cessna waiting for takeoff, Morgan was glad she'd agreed to take ARKANE's help. The plane was set up as a mobile base, with a meeting room and galley up front, and weapons, equipment, and bunks to the rear.

"Why Spain?" Jake asked.

"Before the attack, Ben and I discussed the legends about where the Apostles went after Pentecost. It seems logical that the stones would be kept near the locations of their deaths, either with a Keeper, or preserved with the relics of the saints."

"That makes sense," Jake said, "and it ties with our research as well."

"We should go after the more obvious Apostles first, so I narrowed them down. If I have the stone of John, then Patmos, Greece, is off the list, and it's likely that Faye has James Alphaeus's stone."

Jake nodded. "ARKANE has Matthew Levi's and our researchers think it was Nathaniel's that was taken in Varanasi. The stone of Matthias was stolen from a museum in Istanbul."

"That's five," Morgan added, "and I'm pretty sure Everett already has the stone of Thomas. His father's journal describes the Maltese and Goan myths around where the Doubting Apostle ended up. That accounts for half of them. We just need another six."

She pointed to a corner of northwest Spain on the map in the front of the journal. "The bones of St James are supposedly held at the Cathedral of

Santiago de Compostela. The myths are pretty consistent and it's a short flight, so it's worth starting there."

The destination locked in, Jake and the crew readied for takeoff. As the plane rose above the British countryside, Morgan stared out the window. She had tried to smother her fear with the intellectual rigor of research, but a gaping wound opened up, and she couldn't help the edge of anguish creeping in as she thought of Faye and Gemma.

Picking up her phone, Morgan scrolled to pictures of her family. One of Gemma smiling. Another of Faye, Gemma, and David in the kitchen together, flour dusting her sister's cheek. Morgan pretended to wipe something from her eye, not wanting Jake to see her vulnerability. Elian and her parents had been ripped from her life too soon. She would not lose her sister and niece.

Once they were at cruising altitude, Jake pulled out several more maps with details of their destination. "I thought about doing the Camino de Santiago myself a few years back."

Morgan glanced up, surprised by his words. "To atone for what sins? What could an ARKANE agent possibly have on his conscience?"

The Camino was a thousand-year-old pilgrimage with routes across Europe to the saint's relics. It was traditionally walked on foot as a spiritual journey, culminating at the cathedral of St James in Santiago de Compostela, where the pilgrim received forgiveness for their sin.

Jake smiled broadly, the scar above his eyebrow crinkling. "I haven't always been so squeaky clean."

He traced the streets on the map of Santiago de Compostela and located the main square. His fingers were long, like a piano player's, less calloused than Morgan expected, but there were also old scars on his knuckles, evidence of a harder side.

"It's only an hour or so until we arrive and we won't have long at the cathedral," Jake said. "We need to know what we're looking for. We have to think like those who've protected the stones for generations."

Morgan turned to a page in the journal marked with finely drawn labels and ancient routes marked across modern cities. The world had changed, but they could still follow the footsteps of holy men, even though their fates remained shrouded in mystery.

It was hard to be upbeat about their prospects. One moment Morgan found herself engaged with the research and the next bowled over by the enormity of their task — but she couldn't contemplate failure.

She traced the spidery handwriting on the page with a fingertip. "These diaries are so detailed. Everett's father had so much information and clearly tracked some of the stones. It's odd that he didn't find the rest after all that research."

Jake flashed a grin. "Maybe he just didn't have the right team."

Morgan couldn't help but smile back. They had a long journey ahead of them, and she appreciated his attempt at camaraderie.

They studied the street maps and identified the best route in and out of the cathedral square before settling back for the last stage of the journey.

Jake poured them both another coffee. "It's strange that the Apostles scattered and never regrouped after Pentecost. They had such an intense shared experience and yet it seems they never saw one another again. They couldn't have known their message would spread so successfully throughout the ancient world, even though it meant persecution and martyrdom for them and their followers."

Morgan took a sip of the bitter black. "They had a mission, I suppose. Maybe Pentecost gave them certainty of their authority, or perhaps the power scared them and they scattered, knowing it had to be taken to the far corners of the world?"

She turned to an image in the journal. A page

filled with flames and agonized faces amid dancing fire, thin ink lines with detail of realistic pain, as if drawn from life by a close observer. "Whatever these stones can do, it's not all about healing. Fire has a dark side and it can bring death and destruction, as well as life. Perhaps the power of the Pentecost stones is not something to be taken lightly."

CHAPTER 8

Santiago de Compostela, Spain. May 20

THE PLANE LANDED AT a private airport outside the city. Morgan and Jake took a taxi to the center of town and walked into the Plaza de la Quintana, where the cathedral loomed over the bustling square. Two towers rose up against the skyline, an ancient bastion of faith in a heaving modern city.

"The towers represent James's parents, Zebedee and Maria Salome," Morgan explained as they walked to the cathedral entrance across the plaza.

Pilgrims sat in groups on the paving stones, backpacks and staffs by their sides, clothes dirty from the Way, smiles of pride and relief on their faces.

"I love what Santiago de Compostela represents," Morgan said. "Like you, it's one of my dreams to walk the Camino. I didn't think I would make it here by plane and taxi, though. I hoped to limp in like the rest of the pilgrims."

Jake laughed. "I'm sure you'll hobble through this square one day. What else do you know about the cathedral?"

"Legend tells that James brought the gospel to Spain and, although he was martyred in Jerusalem, his remains were brought back here. The tomb was abandoned in the third century but rediscovered in the ninth by a hermit who saw strange lights in the sky above. A chapel was built to commemorate the miracle of finding the saint's bones and, over generations, it was embellished to become the great cathedral it is today."

"If the relics of James rested here for thousands of years, it should be a good place to search for the stone. At least if it was kept with his bones, that is."

"If they even *are* his bones," Morgan replied. "The Church had an excellent trade in relics, sold as forgiveness for sin to those desperate for a better life after death. Ancient bones of the saints are hardly rare."

They reached the stairs leading up to the entrance of the cathedral, flanked by statues of David and Solomon, wise kings of ancient Israel.

Morgan pointed out the scallop shell carved into the flagstones, the symbol of St James also worn on the staff of the pilgrim. "Legend says that when James's body was transported back to Spain from

Jerusalem, a knight fell into the water and emerged covered in scallop shells. But that sounds like a poor cover-up for the more likely version. The scallop shell was a symbol of fertility carried by hopeful couples and the pagan symbol incorporated into the legend of St James. The early Christians were incredibly effective at integrating pagan ideas. It's why the gospel reached such diverse cultures and spread so widely."

The press of pilgrims intensified as they reached the entrance, as all attempted to fit through the door into the cathedral for mass. Jake reached for Morgan's arm, guiding her inside, keeping her close. She was acutely aware of his touch as they continued deeper into the church, and it felt strangely comforting.

The line of pilgrims snaked through the nave. Morgan pointed past them to the Pórtico da Gloria in the western facade. "The statue of James is back there. We should touch his foot like the other pilgrims and see what else is around."

They walked toward the Romanesque portico. Christ, the Judge and Redeemer, stood in the middle, surrounded by statues of the Apostles and Old Testament figures. Pilgrims surrounded the statue of James, touching or kissing his left foot in a groove worn deep over generations.

The cathedral epitomized the glory of the Catholic Church, but Morgan knew it wasn't the final destination that mattered on the Camino.

It was the journey.

Putting on a backpack each day and heading into the early morning mists of the Way, one foot in front of the other for days on end. A time of contemplation and healing where the only concern was food and water and a bed for the night.

Most people didn't walk the Camino for physical challenge, but as a time to step away from the world and seek answers. Morgan was raised Jewish in Israel, but with her Catholic mother's background, she found herself torn between two great religions, balanced on the edge of both — and belonging to neither.

Perhaps she felt drawn to the Camino as a seeker of spiritual truth, whatever that might mean. Or perhaps it was a way to grieve for a life that could have been with Elian. She wondered why Jake wanted to do it. Morgan knew little about the ARKANE agent, but she didn't expect this tentative partnership to last long enough to find out.

One pilgrim reached out to the foot of St James and wept as he prayed aloud, thanking God for his deliverance. His beard was long and unkempt, and Morgan wondered how far he'd walked to get here.

After living at a level of basic subsistence for many weeks, pilgrims emerged from the rough track to the opulent cathedral.

But could God be found here in gold and marble extravagance, or on the Way in the shadow of stone walls and a swig of fresh water after a long day's walk?

Morgan considered that faith might more likely be found in the sweet relief of taking off walking boots, the stretching of calf muscles, and the respite of sleep, not the communion of saints and the drowning of incense. Even if you didn't find God on the Camino, many found peace — and right now, Morgan wished for just a little of that.

Sudden shouts came from the cloister.

Jake turned to look in the direction of the commotion, but the pilgrims blocked his view. "You concentrate on finding the bones. I'll see what the noise is about."

As he slipped off toward the clamor, Morgan searched for any sign of where the stone of St James might be.

Near the altar, she found a way down into the crypt where the relic bones of the saint were kept. It was a plain staircase, quite incongruous considering the extravagance of sculpture and fresco around it.

At the bottom of the crypt stairs, there was a

small room with a locked iron gate. Morgan peered through the bars into the gloom. The crypt was badly lit, clearly not designed to be part of the tourist route through the cathedral, but she could make out a reliquary of gold and silver on an altar a few meters beyond.

Morgan pushed against the barred gate, but the lock remained solid.

"What do you need, señora?"

Morgan spun around, startled by the sudden voice. An old priest shuffled out of the darkness behind her, his hands shaking with the palsy of age.

"Buenos días, Father. I'm a scholar from the University of Oxford researching the bones of St James. Do you know how I could gain access?"

The old man hobbled forward on his cane, breath wheezing. Morgan helped him to a marble bench by the crypt door.

He patted the seat next to him. "We don't get many people interested in the crypt any more. I'm the Custodian. What would you like to know?"

Morgan wondered if it was wise to talk to this stranger, but time ticked on and there was a lot to be accomplished before Pentecost. Her father taught her to believe that, when it came down to it, most people sought to do good in the world. Those values hadn't saved him, but it certainly made his life a better one.

She sat down on the bench next to the Custodian. "I'm looking for a small stone. It was with St James when he died and may be here in the cathedral."

The old man went pale and clutched at his chest, his wheezing growing worse. "The stone… Who are you really, child?"

Before Morgan could explain, heavy footsteps echoed from the stairs down into the crypt.

Someone was coming.

Morgan tensed. She was trapped down here with no backup and no way out except for the staircase.

A man ducked down to enter the crypt.

Morgan bent her head, as if in prayer, hoping the man was just a tourist and that he would soon move on. She put her hands behind her back anyway, feeling around for anything she could use as a weapon, just in case. She certainly regretted the decision to come unarmed.

"Can I help you, my son?" the priest said softly.

The man turned toward them… and Morgan saw the pale horse tattoo on his left arm.

After leaving Morgan by the pillar of St James, Jake walked toward the cloister, his steps quickening as the noise escalated.

The cathedral was hardly silent, but raised voices attracted attention even amongst a multitude of pilgrims. The cloister was a large quadrangle that led to the cathedral library. Buttressed arches surrounded a tessellated stone pavement, which opened out to the azure Spanish sky.

Three men, clearly ex-military operatives, argued with a gesticulating priest. Faint shapes under their clothes indicated they were armed — and one had a pale horse's head tattoo on his arm.

Thanatos.

Jake had to keep them away from Morgan long enough so she could find the stone, and they could both get out of here.

One man held the priest's arm and pointed into the cathedral nave, clearly demanding that he show them the bones of St James. They would not waste time looking for the stone discreetly. They would use brute force. Pilgrims and other priests stood on the perimeter, but the apparent threat of the three men was enough to keep them at a safe distance.

The invaders headed toward the entrance, pushing the priest in front of them. Jake stood in the shadow of an arch and touched the stone he still wore around his neck. He quickly weighed up his choices, then unhooked it from around his neck.

As they approached, Jake stepped out, holding the

stone in front of him on its leather string. "Looking for this?"

The men pushed the priest to the ground and ran at Jake, drawing their weapons.

He sprinted away into the nave of the cathedral, ducking low behind a group of pilgrims as they entered through the main door. They huddled together, an emotional group intending to finish their journey at the statue of St James.

Jake stayed with them, head bowed, watching out of the corner of his eye.

The attackers scanned the nave, weapons concealed once more. They couldn't risk having their guns out in a such a crowded place. It would be mayhem within seconds and the tourist police were nearby in the square outside.

Jake moved with the pilgrims toward the main altar, aware that Morgan was somewhere close. He didn't want to lead them to her. He needed to create a diversion.

A heavy rope hung down near the main altar — and Jake knew just what he could do to attract everyone's attention.

The cathedral was the home of the most famous Botafumeiro in Christendom, the largest censer in the world, weighing over 170 pounds. On holy days and high mass, it swung over the crowd of pilgrims, trailing a cloud of incense over the gathered faithful. The smoke curled its way up to heaven, carrying prayers to God, bridging the gap between the physical and spiritual realms. On a more practical level, it also served the purpose of masking the stench of pilgrims after days on the trail.

The heavy rope that linked the pulley system to the Botafumeiro was tethered near the main altar. It went right up into the dome above the main crossing of the cathedral, the highest place to swing the censer over the crowd.

One of the attackers spotted Jake.

The men darted through the crowd, hands on concealed weapons, spreading out to flank him near the altar.

Jake rushed to the Botafumeiro rope and drew a knife from his concealed holster. He grabbed the rope, wrapped it around his waist and leg — then slashed the line that held it in place.

Just as the men reached him, the pulley system hoisted Jake up into the dome. Nearby pilgrims watched in wonder as he swung into the air high above the altar. Priests shouted for security and waved their arms, appalled at the sacrilege.

Jake couldn't help but laugh at the sight of them rushing to stop him while he flew above their heads in the dome, rocking his body back and forth, causing the pulley to swing as it would do with the incense.

The three men from Thanatos faded into the crowd, staying back as security and tourist police thronged the cathedral. With their attention on him, Jake could only hope Morgan was having more luck finding the stone of James.

CHAPTER 9

D OWN IN THE CRYPT, the man turned and put his hand inside his jacket pocket. Morgan couldn't let him fire a gun in here. She launched herself at him, springing up and jabbing an elbow into his gut.

He doubled over, and she rammed her knee into his face. His eyes widened in surprise at her attack, but he didn't go down. He pulled a knife from his boot.

Morgan ducked under his arm — just as the old priest rushed in to separate them.

The attacker's knife thrust into the priest's chest and he sagged with a faint exhalation of surprise. Crimson blossomed on his white cassock and he collapsed back on the bench.

Time slowed. Morgan had to finish this now.

She grabbed a heavy Bible and swung it into the attacker's face, smashing his nose and driving him backward. She kicked his wrist. He dropped his knife, leaving a smear of blood on the flagstones.

Morgan ducked under his next clumsy punch and slammed her elbow up under his chin as she reached for a silver candlestick on a ledge just behind the attacker. As his neck snapped back, she swung the candlestick, connecting with the side of his head with a brutal thump.

He collapsed to the floor.

Morgan followed him down, weapon held high to strike again.

A moan from the old priest. "No more, please."

Morgan exhaled, suddenly aware she was in a holy place. She felt for a pulse in the attacker's neck. It was weak, but he was still alive.

She reached inside his jacket and took out his gun, tucking it into the back of her jeans. She pulled the man's belt off, tied his hands, and stuffed one of the ornamental altar pieces into his mouth as a gag.

Morgan knelt next to the old priest and put pressure on his wound, trying to stem the bleeding. The cut wasn't deep, as his voluminous robes had caught the force of the blow, but he was still in a lot of pain.

"I'll get you help soon, but that man was looking for the stone of James. If you know anything, please tell me. You can trust me. I have a stone myself, from John, the beloved disciple."

She reached into her shirt and pulled out her stone pendant. The old priest reached up and touched it gently, his eyes bright with wonder and reverence despite his pain.

"La Piedra de Dios," he whispered. "The stones have been protected by only a few through millennia, but I heard rumors of a reckoning. There's a prophecy that speaks of a new Pentecost in the end times."

"I don't know if this is that time, Father, but I need to find it and I need to get you some help. Let me call someone."

The priest shook his head. "Not yet. If others come, you won't be able to take the stone from the crypt."

Morgan frowned. "It's here?"

The priest gazed into the darkness of the crypt. "I'm clearly no longer capable of protecting it, but will you keep it safe for the Church?"

She hesitated and spoke honestly. "I'm not a Christian, Father, and my sister's life is at stake. I need the stones to get her back."

He sighed. "You're a Keeper, and the stones know their masters. It is enough."

He pointed at the gold and silver reliquary behind the locked gate with a shaky hand. "It's in there. I've never seen it, but Pope Leo XIII authenticated the relics in 1884. My great-great-grandfather was a silversmith and fashioned the reliquary to protect the relics and hide the stone."

The priest crossed himself, his eyes haunted. "Pope Leo had a vision that year which shook him deeply. He heard the voices of God and the Devil while praying at his private altar. Satan boasted that, given a hundred years, he could destroy the Church and gain absolute power over the faithful. God would allow Satan to do his worst as he did with the prophet, Job. But Pope Leo was determined to bolster the Church's power and ensure that the Devil didn't claw a foothold. Hiding the Pentecost stone was just one thing he did to protect the Church from those who would use its power for evil."

The priest slipped one hand into his vestments and pulled out a key. He handed it to Morgan and waved her toward the locked gate. "The stone is molded into the top of the reliquary."

Morgan unlocked the gate and pushed the creaking door inward. A large engraved silver chest rested on top of a mahogany table in the center of the crypt, before an altar flanked by candlesticks.

"On the sides of the box are scallop shells," the old man called faintly from behind. "Count three in from the left."

Morgan followed his directions as he continued. "Follow the seam to the figure underneath. That's the servant of James, the first Keeper. He holds the key to the stone. That's all my father told me, passed down from his father before him."

Morgan examined the silver casting. The figure looked similar to the other molded statues on the side of the reliquary. But as she bent closer, she could see something different about his staff.

She carefully pried it out of the servant's hands. It was a finely tooled sliver of metal, like a needle with a hooked end shaped like a scallop shell. She ran her fingers over the raised dials on the top of the box, acutely aware that they might contain one of the most holy relics in Christendom.

There was a tiny hole in the dial on the left and Morgan pressed the metal shard into the little space. It slid in snugly, but nothing happened. She wiggled it and lifted it like a lever.

The silver dial opened smoothly to reveal a plain grey stone in the space beneath.

"It's here," Morgan whispered.

She gently lifted the stone out of its hiding place and closed the lid with care. She removed the tiny silver lever, returned it to the servant, and walked back out into the crypt.

The old priest held out his hand. "Please let me see

it. I've spent so many years protecting its location."

Morgan knelt by his side and laid the stone on his palm. It was plain, a dark grey with rough edges. Nothing out of the ordinary. While her own was carved into jewelry, this one looked as clean as the day it was hacked from the tomb of Christ.

The old man closed his hand around the precious object, his eyes closed in prayer.

Shouts came from above them in the nave.

The old priest gave a hacking cough, and he clutched at his wound, blood staining the stone.

He gave it back to Morgan. "Go now. The other priests will find me soon enough and I'll explain this mess. Be careful, child."

"Thank you. I'll keep it safe." Morgan turned and ran up the stairs, leaving the old priest in the darkness below.

When she reached the nave, she saw what all the noise was about. Jake was suspended in the dome, swinging on a thick rope and laughing maniacally, playing the part of the crazy pilgrim to perfection.

After her experience in the crypt, she could only think that he'd had a run-in with other men from Thanatos and found a unique way to handle the situation. Morgan looked up at him from the gathered crowd, grateful that he could make her smile despite the situation. He was a good partner to have around for now, whatever ARKANE's ultimate motives might be.

But they needed to get out of here.

The Holy Door of the Pardon stood unguarded while the security guards clamored to bring Jake down from the dome. They would retrieve him soon enough, so Morgan needed to get his attention while he was still high up.

The Holy Door was only opened in holy years, when the feast day of St James fell on a Sunday. This was not a holy year, so opening the door would certainly attract attention. More people flocked into the nave to witness the spectacle and the security team was surrounded by crowds, so they wouldn't have time to reach her before she was away.

Morgan made her decision.

She hurried over to the Holy Door, pulled the attacker's gun from her waistband, and shot the ancient lock.

The sharp bang and splintering of wood drew screams in the church — and certainly got Jake's attention.

Morgan yanked the door open and ran out, disappearing into the back streets of Santiago de Compostela.

A few hours later, Jake arrived back at the airport in a Spanish police vehicle and bounded up the steps onto the plane.

Morgan sat with her feet up, reading one of the Moleskine journals, a mug of coffee in one hand.

Jake grinned. "Glad to see you were so worried about me. Nice diversion with the Holy Door, by the way. You should have seen the faces of the priests as you left, and I swung above them in the dome. All their worst nightmares at once."

"I think the pilgrims will suffer enhanced security from now on," Morgan replied with a smile, sitting forward in her chair.

Jake scanned Morgan for injuries, more worried than he wanted to admit. "The police mentioned there was a stabbing in the crypt. Are you okay?"

Morgan pulled the stone from her pocket and handed it to Jake. "One of the Thanatos guys dropped in, but he wasn't a problem for long." She pointed out the plain rock. "This one is somehow more authentic. There's no decoration or carving like the others."

Jake examined it. "Do you think we should sense something since we have three stones in one place? Should we be speaking in tongues or healing the masses?"

Morgan chuckled as she took the stone back and tucked it away deep in her jacket pocket. "You believe that about as much as I do, but we still need the others. Whatever they can do, we need to hurry for Faye and Gemma's sake."

"I know how important they are to you." Jake put his hand over Morgan's and their eyes locked for just a moment, a current of connection between them.

She pulled her hand from his and looked away.

A curl of dark hair hung down across her face and Morgan brushed it back behind her ear, her skin luminous from the Spanish sun shining through the plane window. Jake had known she would get back from the cathedral with no problems. When the Holy Door creaked open and Morgan dashed out, he slid back down the rope and let the police take him away before Marietti cleared up the situation.

Jake knew that he and Morgan made a good team, and her ease in dealing with the fight in the crypt made him even more sure of that. Clearly, she could look after herself — and that confidence made her strangely unapproachable. He hadn't met a woman like her in a long time.

"I need to speak to Marietti and report back," he said. "Maybe we can get some help with our next location."

"Go ahead." Morgan bent to the journal once more, cross-referencing it with the information Ben had provided.

Jake walked into the small pilot's area and put in a call to Marietti.

The director was curt. "Do you have the stone of James?"

"Yes. Morgan found it, but a team from Thanatos was there to intercept. They may still follow us, so we need to move on quickly."

"We've had intel there's a bounty out on you two, so it's likely you'll be followed all the way. You must stop those stones falling into the wrong hands, Jake — whatever it takes. Talk to Martin now. He has your next destination."

Jake walked back into the main cabin and switched to speakerphone, gesturing for Morgan to listen in. "Hey, Spooky, what have you got for us?"

The line crackled a little, but Martin's enthusiasm was clear. "The stone of Thaddeus — I think it's in northern Iran."

Morgan leaned forward. "There was an early church community in Persia, but why would a stone be hidden there?"

Martin outlined his research. "You're right, Christianity was established early in Persia, now Iran. Some of those who heard the Apostles speak on Pentecost were Persian, and they took the gospel back with them and started the church there. The Apostle Thaddeus, also known as Jude, is venerated as one of the founders and patron saints. Despite its modern reputation for intolerance and Islamic fundamentalism, Persia was at the forefront of culture for millennia."

Morgan nodded. "I see what you mean. Christians have been persecuted there, but ancient churches remain. Iran has some incredible archaeological treasures, but it's not exactly a tourist destination these days."

Martin continued, "The Armenian Apostolic Church is one of the oldest Christian communities in the world, with religious authority stretching far beyond their territory. Armenia was also the first country to adopt Christianity as its official religion in 301 AD, tracing its origins to the Apostles. The Armenian Church followed its own path, officially splitting with Rome and Constantinople in 554 after rejecting the position of the Church at Chalcedon."

Jake looked a little lost at the finer points of Christian history, so Morgan explained, "Chalcedon was a turning point in early Church history with differences in belief causing a schism between east and west."

The line crackled before Martin cut back in.

"The Armenians and Eastern Orthodox believe in one incarnate nature of Christ, uniting human and divine, whereas the Roman Church believed in a dual nature — human and divine as separate. The Armenians still have claim to a part of ancient Jerusalem and one of their Patriarchs resides there. Persians also have a long history in the Bible, with Cyrus the Great, Cambyses, and Darius all mentioned. The area around Tabriz, in northern Iran near the border with Armenia, is also thought to be the location of the biblical Eden."

Morgan tilted her head to one side, frowning a little. "We don't have any other solid leads right now, so it's worth a try."

"Okay, Martin," Jake said. "Can you email that over and we'll review on the way?"

"Sure, but be careful over there. Thaddeus is the patron saint of lost causes and desperate situations. Make sure you don't need his help. Good luck." He hung up.

Jake looked at Morgan. "Guess it's Iran next. I'll sort out the clearance."

After checking in with the flight crew, Jake went back into the cabin to find Morgan curled up asleep in her recliner chair.

Concern creased her face, and Jake knew she worried about her family. For a moment, he was struck with jealousy. He had no family to worry about anymore, and no one to care about what happened to him. Had he really allowed himself to become so isolated? Or had his lifestyle at ARKANE prevented any lasting relationships from flourishing?

He shook his head. There was never any time to change things in between the increasing frequency of missions. It seemed the world erupted with global threats on a weekly basis. At least they had a few hours to rest before they arrived in Iran.

Jake pulled down one of the flight blankets and draped it gently around Morgan. She stirred a little and then settled back, her face more relaxed. He sat down in his chair, a frown creasing his forehead as he considered the challenge ahead.

CHAPTER 10

Tucson, Arizona, USA. May 20

JOSEPH EVERETT SAT IN the chair his father had loved more than his children. The leather still creaked with the same tone it had when the old man reached for another book. He and Michael listened to it over and over as they huddled with ears pressed to the always-closed study door. Joseph had recreated that study here within his own house, sure that the secret to his father's quest lay within the pages of one of these books.

He sat behind a large teak desk inlaid with rose marble around the edges. An accountant's lamp with a green hood and a pull-down switch sat on the corner of the desk next to his father's precious collection of fountain pens. Joseph examined the red Montegrappa pen, always pride of place on his father's desk. He had been beaten for touching it as a child, but he still found it beautiful with its rich color and intricately carved nib. It was truly a piece of art.

Five years ago, his father lay in the final throes of lung cancer, coughing up blood and bile onto a stained bedspread. The air smelt of vomit and death crept around the walls, waiting for the inevitable end.

His father had unhooked the stone pendant from around his mottled neck and handed it to Joseph, whispering in halting speech.

"This is a Pentecost stone…" The dying man broke off in a coughing fit, then spoke again, his words even fainter. "There are more… Death increases their power. Find them all. Finish my work."

He slipped into a coma soon after, and Joseph held the stone, feeling the warmth from his father's body leave it for the final time. He didn't know what the words meant then. It was just a piece of rock — but it was the only thing his father had ever given him.

After the funeral, Joseph rifled through his father's study and began to read his diaries, along with journal articles about the Apostles. He searched every day for information on where the stones might be and how to energize them when they were together once more. Scraps of cuttings from obscure fringe publications filled the diaries, the chronology of a mind over years of historical and supernatural research.

It was in these pages that Joseph found vital information about the estimated dating of the comet's return on Pentecost this year. It had given him a timeframe to work to, but he hadn't thought it would take so long to achieve his goal. Now time was running out.

The diary also contained experiments his father carried out, noting that the energy transfer of death could increase the power of the stone. The nun's fiery end at Varanasi had certainly released miracles in a pillar of flame.

If only he could have tested the hypothesis with his first murder. The one that still meant the most to him.

After his father's funeral, his mother had sat in the kitchen, bulging blue veins visible in her thick legs. The author of the brothers' misery, squatting like a toad over their lives. Joseph flinched as she slurped from a cup of tea. He hated the sound of her drinking, the sound of her living.

That night, he went to her room and held a pillow over her face. He held her down easily, resting his weight on top of her until the struggling stopped.

He wept then, for the end of whatever it was people called family. But now it was just him and Michael against the world. Perhaps it had always been that way.

Joseph bent down, placed the red Montegrappa pen on the floor, and crushed it underfoot. He ground the pieces into the carpet, purple ink staining the cream weave, spreading out like a bloodstain.

The past was over. It was time to move forward. He would find a way to test the theory that death empowered the stones.

Tucson, Arizona, USA. May 20.

As darkness fell, José Ramirez pulled the thread-bare blanket closer and curled into the doorway, trying to make himself invisible.

He had walked most of the day, always moving, to avoid the police, who seemed to be on every corner. He tried to cultivate an air of going somewhere, of being on an errand, because he couldn't seem journey-less. Arizona was cracking down on illegal immigrants, but how did America expect them to stop coming when there was opportunity here, even if you had to fight to get it?

José had spent his last coins on a meal earlier and didn't know how he would eat tomorrow. Maybe his cousin would help — if he could make it that far north. At least the Tucson streets were warm enough to make waking up tomorrow a more likely event.

As sleep eased him away from the hard ground beneath, a vehicle pulled up next to the curb, engine idling. José lay motionless, praying it was not the police or immigration come to take him away. If he stayed still, perhaps they wouldn't notice him.

A car door slammed. Footsteps approached his doorway.

José sat up and scrambled to his feet, ready to run.

The man standing in front of him didn't look like a cop. His hair was too long, his clothes more desert dirt bike than law enforcement. The van behind him had Tucson State Shelter stenciled on the side.

"Do you need somewhere to stay? We have a shelter and food for the night. You shouldn't be on the streets."

José shook his head. "I'm alright here. I'll move on tomorrow. Thanks for the offer, though."

The man shrugged. "Of course, if you're sure. But there may be work tomorrow if you come with us. We have some construction going on at the shelter."

José considered his options. He really needed the money. He pushed down his nagging doubts, picked up his blanket and meager bag of possessions, and walked toward the van.

The man opened the back and waved him inside.

José realized his mistake as soon as the door shut behind him.

Someone grabbed him in the dark and slammed José down on the floor. He struggled, shouting as the van drove off. But there was no one to hear him on the street outside, and security cameras would only show a homeless man helped to shelter for the night.

He felt the sting of a needle in his neck, and the world faded to black.

No one would report him missing. No one even knew he was there.

José woke to the dull thunk of an axe biting into wood. It was a sound he knew well from his childhood in Mexico, where he cut wood for the cooking fire with his father.

His head was fuzzy, but he could feel his hands tied behind him and his feet secured tightly. José opened his eyes.

He was strapped to a wooden post with stacked firewood around his legs. He was gagged, the stink of smoke and some other rank smell on the material.

A man watched him from beyond the pyre. He

was expensively dressed, like a businessman, and he caressed a stone in the palm of his hand.

"The Lord's fire purifies as well as destroys," he said. "Fire has been used for ritual sacrifice to many gods throughout the ages. Martyrs of the Christian faith died this way, and it was a favored instrument of mercy in the auto-da-fé of the Spanish Inquisition. You are in esteemed company, my friend."

Another man piled up smaller logs and kindling at the base of the pyre, stacking it close. José struggled against his bonds and screamed against the gag.

The businessman leaned in and put the stone, strung on a chain, over José's head. It hung against his chest, a heavy weight with a coolness that would soon turn to searing pain.

The other man approached with a can of gasoline, sloshing it over the bound sacrifice and the pile of wood beneath.

José struggled once more in his bonds, seeing his death upon him, terrified of the pain to come. He prayed desperately for some miracle to save him.

The click of a lighter. The whoosh of flame.

The fire grew quickly, catching on the gasoline, exploding into tongues of flame, engulfing José.

His skin burned and he howled into the gag as agony spread, obliterating his consciousness. He died with a last prayer on his blackened lips.

Joseph Everett watched the flesh on the vagrant's body burn through as the fire raged. He held a wet cloth over his mouth and nose to block the stench as he waited for the moment the man died, his spirit transfigured into smoke. The stone glowed around the corpse's neck, burning bright gold, lit by dancing flame.

Once the fire was only embers and ash, Joseph leaned over the burnt chest cavity and pulled the stone out from the remains. He didn't touch it directly, but wrapped it in a pure white linen cloth, feeling the last of its warmth.

Joseph drove out in the dawn, back to the hospital, leaving his men to clean up the mess. Perhaps this time, he might see a glimmer of response in Michael's eyes.

CHAPTER 11

Tabriz, Iran. May 21

MORGAN FOLLOWED JAKE THROUGH the main bazaar of Tabriz, a full-length burqa hiding both her body and her weapons. Jake walked briskly in front, without looking back, as a man should in this part of the world.

The bazaar had high domed ceilings of red brick studded with star-shaped skylights that let in piercing shafts of light. Koranic verses in deep indigo decorated some arches, overlaid with pearly Arabic script and gold patterns set back in the niches.

Shops lined the passageways with goods spilling out on to the footpath, hinting at more treasures inside. Sacks overflowed with grain and spices, dates and walnuts, apricots and almonds. Piles of scented soap lay heaped up next to oil paintings, bright clothing hung from doorways, and gold glittered in the jewelry shops while the blistering sun streamed down through the skylights. Men smoked sheesha pipes and drank mint tea together as they played chess in the cafés. Women chatted in anonymous groups, hidden in full-length black.

It was a busy hub of commerce, fascinating at every turn, and Morgan would have lingered under different circumstances, her fingers trailing over silk, the scent of jasmine and cinnamon in the air.

But there was no time for that now.

The muezzin's call to prayer echoed through the bazaar. The faithful threw down their mats and prayed with the imam. Jake hesitated briefly, but others scurried past, ignoring the devotion, so they continued deeper into the souk.

It was Morgan's first experience of Iran, and certainly not the way she had expected to see it. Tabriz was a mottled azure city, colorful and busy with architecture from millennia ago to skyscrapers of the industrial age. An archaeological paradise few could visit because centuries of invasion, war, and neglect had left the ruins so inaccessible.

They headed for the church of St Mary, considered the second-oldest church in the world after the Church of the Nativity in Bethlehem. Built in the twelfth century, it was the seat of the Archbishop of the Armenian Church. Marco Polo even mentioned it in his travels. The church was built over an Armenian holy place, with some rocks as old as faith itself.

They entered the tiny square in front of the church with its lofty tower and ancient bronze bell. A rough-hewn rope hung down, ready for ringing, but it was quiet today, a silent witness to an ancient faith practiced in an overwhelmingly Muslim country.

Morgan and Jake approached the front portico of the church and stooped to enter the small door set with large wooden panels.

A heavy scent of incense overwhelmed Morgan as she blinked in the dark interior, eyes adjusting to the dim light. The cool air was welcoming after the harsh heat outside. The church was simple at first glance, with wooden seats facing a basic altar, but when she looked more closely, Morgan noticed frescoes of ecclesiastical figures on the walls.

"Stay here," Jake whispered. "I'll talk to the priest." He walked down the aisle toward a robed figure tending the altar near the front of the church.

Through the veil shielding her face, Morgan looked around the church for some symbol of the Apostles. Coming here was a long shot, but the Armenian Church was one of the most ancient and the apostolic succession was precious to their faith. It was possible a stone could be here.

Jake returned quickly. "There's a shrine to the Apostle Thaddeus at the side of the church. Follow me."

He walked away, and Morgan followed closely, her head down in a modest pose as they entered the shrine.

Graphic images from the Passion of Christ covered the walls, as well as the deaths of the saints depicted in excruciating detail. One panel showed Simon the Zealot hacked in half with a long saw while crowds jeered at his death. His face was bright and shining; a halo lit his features. He showed no pain, even though blood spurted from his side.

Opposite was St Peter's crucifixion in Rome, upside down at his own request because he didn't deserve to die in the same way as his savior.

A large stained-glass window illuminated the chapel, intricately decorated with more symbols of the saints.

Morgan quickly scanned the side panels, looking for any sign of Thaddeus.

She found the figure of the Apostle on the western side, recognizable by his club. "Jake, look at this. There are flames around his head, but it's as if he's above all suffering. He's even wearing a stone." The pendant seemed to be raised above the rest of the painting. "Do you think it's actually in there under the paint?"

"It might be, but we have little time, so you'd better work fast."

He guarded the doorway, and Morgan hoisted up her burqa, revealing a tool belt underneath, along with a couple of handguns. She took out a tiny metal file and sawed around the bump in the panel, careful to cut close so as not to disturb too much of the fresco. The disturbing image of Simon's bloody torso just to her left made her shudder. His faith and dedication led him to torture and death. Would she be able to suffer that much for her family?

Morgan continued etching and, as the paint flaked away, she recognized the patina of the stone beneath matched the others. At least they were in the right place.

Jake's low whistle broke her concentration, and she looked behind to see him frantically motioning her to stop and join him.

A group of men in military uniform stood by the door of the church, speaking to the priest.

"I recognize the leader from the cathedral in Spain," Jake whispered. "They must have tracked us here."

Morgan handed him a gun. "You need to hold them off. We can't leave the stone here."

Hurrying back to the fresco, she cut more quickly, less worried about preserving the painting and more concerned with getting out of there alive.

"Hurry," Jake whispered. "We're about to have company." He slowly pushed the heavy door, closing it inch by inch as quietly as possible.

Morgan poked the file under the stone, trying desperately to lever it out. "I've just about got it. Give me one more minute." Flakes of paint lodged in her fingernails as she scratched at the broken surface.

"I don't think we have another minute." Jake pushed the heavy door closed and fumbled with the bolts.

Bullets pinged off the ancient door as the men outside the chapel opened fire.

Jake crouched next to the doorway, protected by the thick walls. "Hurry, they'll blow this door open in no time."

"I've got it." Morgan prized the stone loose from the neck of Thaddeus. It was covered with bits of paint, but she could still make out the carvings. It looked like the same rock as her own stone. She tucked it deep into her tool belt, securing it under her robe. "Let's get out of here."

Jake pointed up at the stained-glass window. "There's no way out of this chapel — except through that."

"You know we're going to hell for desecrating a church." Morgan gave a wry smile. "Just make sure you only shoot out a few panels."

The door rattled as the men from Thanatos slammed into it, using a pew as a battering ram.

Jake indicated the window. "As soon as we're out, let's split up and meet back at the plane. Are you good with that?"

Morgan nodded. "Of course. It's easier for me to get lost in the crowd. I'm more worried about you. You don't exactly fit in around here."

Jake laughed. "I'll be fine. Time to go."

He raised his gun and shot several times into the bottom panel of the stained glass window. As the glass shattered, Jake jumped onto the altar and used a candlestick to smash the final shards away.

Morgan clambered up through the hole, using her robe as a cushion against the broken glass, and dropped the short distance onto the street outside.

The commotion in the church had attracted a crowd, and they gazed curiously at the pair as Jake jumped down beside her.

"See you on the plane." Morgan slipped away into the crowd, blending into a group of veiled women for a block, then ducking into a fabric shop. As she pretended to browse, Morgan breathed a sigh of relief. The men pursuing her would not risk stopping veiled women on the streets. This was a strict Muslim city and they would be punished for harassment.

She was safe — she could only hope that Jake wasn't in too much trouble.

Jake slipped away from the church, but people turned and stared at him, some pointing out his route. It wouldn't be long before the men from Thanatos were on his trail.

He ran into the bazaar, turning corner after corner. But he didn't know the place and attracted attention with his Western looks.

Shouting came from behind him.

Jake ducked into a barber's shop, nestled in the side of the souk.

The barber was busy shaving a customer, and several cut-throat razors lay on a table beside him. Jake pulled out a pile of US dollar notes and shoved them at the barber as he picked up a razor and ducked out the back of the shop.

Jake waited outside the back door, knowing the attackers would soon be upon him.

Voices in the shop turned to angry shouting.

The barber would surely point out the back.

More voices, closer now. There were two men, at least.

Jake tensed, ready to strike.

One man came out, then a second, both striding away from him into the alley behind the shop. They clearly didn't expect him to be waiting for them.

He grabbed the second man from behind and sliced across his throat with the razor. The man didn't even have time to scream.

Blood spurted over Jake's arm. As the body dropped, he shoved it into the back of the first man, ripping the gun from his hand and firing it into his head — once, twice.

It was over in less than a minute.

Jake's breath came heavy and fast. He slowed it purposefully, calming the adrenalin rush. He had not killed in a while, but his pent-up anger and knowledge of what these men would have done to him and Morgan left him no choice. There was too much at stake to let them live, and they would not have given him mercy.

He ran down the alley, away from the bodies and back toward the plane. Marietti would have some cleaning up to do, as Jake's prints would be on the razor and people had seen his face. Luckily, ARKANE had connections that made these issues go away. They also provided a priest for confession if team members needed it.

Jake didn't.

He had made his peace with death a long time ago,

after identifying the bodies of his butchered family in Walkerville, near Johannesburg in South Africa. After he revenged their deaths in a silent bloody rampage, Jake needed an outlet for his rage and grief. His mother's British passport enabled him to join the British military, and he soon rose through the ranks until that fateful night he encountered Marietti.

Jake didn't shy from killing if the mission demanded it — and he didn't need to talk about it afterward. Life was brutal and there were no prizes except to stay alive.

CHAPTER 12 

Tucson, Arizona, USA. May 21

JOSEPH EVERETT PACED BACK and forth across his study as he scoured the ancient text of *On the Martyrs* by Eusebius for insights into holy death. There were inventive ways of killing people in those early centuries. Faced with such horrific ends, Christians became fanatic about their faith, valuing it more as the price of belief was so high. The violence and blood of martyrdom accelerated the growth of the Church — but might it also have enhanced the power of the artifacts?

After the death of the homeless man, Joseph took the stone to Michael and put it around his brother's neck. There might have been a momentary glimmer of fire in those dead eyes, but nothing more. Perhaps the suffering had not been enough. Perhaps he just needed all the stones.

Joseph needed to remind Morgan Sierra of what was at stake and how high the cost could be if she didn't complete her task.

He dialed a number on his phone. "Take the woman out to the desert, but leave the child."

He made another call to his property manager. "Start the fire in the kiln. We're driving out now. See you in a few hours."

Joseph's fascination with flame went back to his teens, a pyromania that fed his soul. A tiny spark could grow to consume entire cities, carving a path for new life in the wake of the old — creation in destruction. He loved the story in the book of Daniel, where the faithful walked in the furnace with angels and emerged triumphant and unscathed.

He found arson as a young man, but the risk of prosecution became too great as his business and political ambitions grew. He devoured details of mass cremation at Auschwitz. The Nazis were experts on disposal of physical evidence, and Joseph had learned how fire could hide his dark deeds. So he directed his addiction into firing pottery in traditional flame kilns, a socially acceptable way to indulge his visceral need. He loved the alchemy of color and the fiery transformation of matter itself. Now the kiln might be the key to accelerating the next phase of his plan.

Joseph headed out in his four-wheel drive to the desert scrubland southwest of Tucson, far away from the city and desolate enough that no one would even want to trespass. The land was technically owned by one of his subsidiary businesses, buried in untraceable shell companies.

As he drove, Joseph thought of Michael in the hospital, listless in his bed, his limbs increasingly withered. He shook his head to clear the thoughts. He shouldn't focus on the past, only on the future.

He smiled, his mirrored sunglasses flashing in the harsh Arizona sun. He had faith in business and money and increasingly in an ancient power. Not a personal Jesus, but a primal energy that raised the dead, brought fire and wind to earth on Pentecost, and burned the early Church into the consciousness of millennia. He would call this power back to earth soon enough.

Once out in the desert, Joseph pulled up to the small workshop a few hundred meters from the oversized kiln. Parked nearby was another car, where two of his men waited in the air-conditioned interior with the woman, Faye, tied and gagged.

The men emerged from the car as Joseph approached.

"Take the rest of the wood to the kiln and stoke it up," he said. "I need it burning at its hottest today. I have a special firing in mind."

As the men went about their task, Joseph opened the car door. Faye was shaking, but her eyes were defiant.

She turned her head away as Joseph reached toward her, the only motion she could manage in her constrained state. He grabbed her hair and pulled it savagely back, exposing her throat.

"You cannot escape your fate — and your sister is going to watch."

Joseph released her, then bent to pick up a hefty rock from the ground, tossing it in his hand as he walked away from the car and joined his men by the kiln. It was the size of a large cupboard with shelves for pots, but with room for a person in the middle of the space to make it easier to stack. There was a thick glass window in the door to watch the process. It took hours to build the temperature high enough for firing, but at that point, the flames would burn blue and bright.

It was almost ready now.

Joseph set up a video camera at the front of the kiln, turned it on, and then motioned for the men to bring Faye.

She struggled and screamed into her gag. One man picked her up and carried her, kicking all the way. They tied her to a chair facing the door of the kiln. Tears ran down her cheeks, and she shook with terror.

Joseph bent down to her ear. "This is what happens if your sister doesn't bring the stones to me by Pentecost."

He whipped around quickly, smashing the rock in his hand into the face of the man who carried Faye over.

The man fell to his knees, briefly stunned.

He shook his head, trying to clear it as blood poured from his nose. Joseph kicked him, his boot connecting with a thud.

The man fell back on the ground, confusion clouding his eyes as he rolled to try and escape.

Joseph moved in for another kick, his heavy boot audibly breaking the man's ribs before stomping down on his temple. The man went limp, his blood staining the earth.

Joseph gestured to the other man. "Help me with this."

Together, they opened the kiln and threw the dazed victim inside, slamming the door again and trapping him inside. The flames roared as they sucked in oxygen from the air.

Joseph held Faye's head in a tight grip, forcing her to watch as the camera recorded everything.

The man's brief screams were terrible as the fire caught. He seemed to dance in the blue and orange haze before falling to his knees, curling up on the floor as the flames consumed him.

"Imagine the lick of that tiny tongue of flame along your skin. It looks so gentle, but that blue-orange dancer is pain and death, its caress the last pleasure you would feel in this life."

Joseph wound his fingers through her hair as tears ran down her face, soaking the gag that choked her.

"Like this man, the saints were burned alive and the smoke from their corpses crossed the boundary between earth and heaven. Fire is humanity's most precious gift. Prometheus stole it from Zeus and transformed us from bestial need to higher thought."

Joseph stood tall in front of the camera, taking the stance of a preacher before his church as Faye cowered beneath his upraised arms.

"Volcanoes brim with fire and Vulcan works there, shaping weapons for the gods from an ever-shifting molten core that will one day overtake us with destruction. Yet the phoenix rises from these flames, a mythical spirit with wings of gold and scarlet. A sign of resurrection rising from destruction, a continuing cycle of rebirth from ancient to ancient again."

He broke off and pointed at Faye, who wept on the ground.

"The Pentecost stones will bring resurrection to my brother and a renaissance in faith and miracles.

Bring them to me — or she will be my next sacrifice to the god of flame."

As the sound of Faye's sobbing filled the air, Joseph fell silent and stared into the fiery kiln. There were no angels in the fire today, only djinn of dirty smoke. The glaze on the pots would be stained with dark red, russet like the desert earth — and the blood of sacrifice.

CHAPTER 13

St Peter's Basilica. Vatican City, Italy. May 22.

MORGAN AND JAKE STOOD on the Ponte de Castel Sant'Angelo, looking over the Tiber toward the cupola of St Peter's. They both held steaming cups of black coffee, dark circles under their eyes.

Neither had slept on the plane from Iran to Italy — not after receiving the video. Morgan couldn't stop thinking about the flames consuming that body in the kiln. For the first few seconds, she thought it was Faye and her heart almost thumped from her chest. Then the camera panned down to her sister huddled in fear, tied and gagged, the reflection of flames flickering in her eyes as Everett ranted at the screen.

The knowledge that time ticked away ever faster tempered Morgan's relief. After Tabriz, she thought that perhaps that the stones they already had would be enough to bargain for the lives of her sister and niece, but the video made it clear she needed to find them all.

There would be no bargaining — and they were running out of time.

Rome, the parish of the Holy Father, home of the Catholic Church, was the obvious next step. The myth of the stones emphasized a spiritual gift of enhanced creativity, and surely this place was the pinnacle of artistic creative expression. Peter was the Rock of the Church and the iconography of stone was deeply bound into the Vatican, a persistent theme in the art and architecture of the ancient city within a city. The stone of St Peter would likely be kept in the basilica named after the saint. But where in the huge Vatican complex might it be?

Morgan turned to look up at the papal fortress and the tomb of the Roman Emperor Hadrian towering above them. The Passetto di Borgo linked the castle to the Vatican with a covered, fortified tunnel. But today they would not steal secretly through a back entrance. They would walk straight in the front door.

The faithful came from all over the world to see *il Papa*, and twice a week he performed mass in the magnificent church. Lines to enter the basilica started around ten, when day trippers arrived, but

Morgan and Jake would enter early to avoid the queues.

The replica of Bernini's *Angel with the Crown of Thorns* gazed down at them with blank eyes. Bernini was the final architect of St Peter's and his vision completed the dome after Bramante, Raphael, and Michelangelo. He was recognized as a creative genius, touched by divine power. Perhaps he had even been one in a long line of Keepers. Their best chance was to follow Bernini's creations.

Morgan and Jake walked the short distance from the bridge up the Via della Conciliazione to the grand oval of Piazza San Pietro.

One hundred and forty saints watched over the pilgrims from the tops of the colonnades surrounding the piazza, men and women of faith throughout the ages, many martyred and standing here as testimony to the power of their God. Bernini designed these colonnades along with the fountain in the forecourt, but it was the ancient red granite obelisk that dominated the piazza. Dating back to the fifth dynasty of ancient Egypt, it had been brought to Rome by the Emperor Augustus and was the only obelisk from ancient times still standing.

Morgan and Jake walked to the tourist entrance of the basilica, waited in line for a short time, and passed easily through security at the gates.

They walked under the colonnade and past the Swiss Guards in their red, yellow, and blue striped tunics, then filed into the church with other worshippers, past the statue of Moses with the Ten Commandments, up the steps, and into the imposing basilica.

Pilgrims from myriad nations prayed and wept at the culmination of their journey to the center of the Christian world.

The scent of incense filled the air, dispersing in clouds toward the dome of Michelangelo, reminding Morgan of the cathedral in Santiago de Compostela. A smile flickered across Jake's face and she could see he was thinking about it too, but there would be no attention-drawing stunts here. This time, they needed to remain unnoticed.

They walked into the main nave, past the groups of people waiting for seats while others thronged the aisles trying to find the best position to see the Pope when he entered. Michelangelo's *Pietà* sat in a niche by the door. The lips of the Virgin were soft, almost pliant, lifelike even in marble. She barely looked the age of her dead son.

From her study of ancient religion, Morgan noticed the influence of ancient Roman polytheism incorporated into the Catholic Church. The statues of previous popes sat as gods on podiums with the faithful at their feet, praying for intercession. The cadavers of some popes lay embalmed behind glass so believers could look upon them and pray for their eternal souls. It was a masterful display of power and faith on every level.

The choir broke into the Magnificat, announcing the beginning of the pre-service, aimed at settling the crowd and instilling a sense of devotion before the Pope entered.

As the pure notes rose up into the dome, Morgan appreciated the song. She often sought peace within the walls of Blackfriars chapel during choir practice, and part of her wanted to stop by one of the soaring columns and listen for just a minute. But Jake motioned for her to follow. They had two places to check for the stone and little time to do it in.

Morgan looked at her watch. It wouldn't be long until the Pope entered for mass.

They made their way through the praying crowd to the tomb of Pope Pius X, his body lying behind glass near the front of the basilica in the eastern wing. His corpse had been disinterred and was remarkably well preserved, despite not being embalmed. It was said to be a miracle and other wonders apparently occurred at his tomb. It was possible that this Pope had been a Keeper of the stone. Perhaps it was even buried with him.

Morgan and Jake knelt in front of the tomb and bent their heads as if to pray, looking over clasped hands into the glass and bronze sarcophagus.

"There's something around his neck," Morgan whispered and glanced up at the Swiss Guard nearby. "But I can't tell from here. How can we get closer?"

"You need to be more religious," Jake whispered back, before flinging himself at the sainted figure, prostrating himself in a fit of enthusiastic prayer.

Jake pressed his face close to the glass before the Swiss Guard on duty hauled him back.

"*Scusi, scusi*," Jake apologized, his hands out in supplication. The guard let him go, but watched warily as Jake knelt back down.

"It's an amulet of sorts, but not the Pentecost stone. If it's in there with him, we'd need better access, anyway. There's no way to break the glass. Let's try the Alexander monument."

Making the sign of the cross as they backed away, Morgan and Jake weaved slowly across the church to Bernini's final masterpiece in St Peter's, the mausoleum of Pope Alexander VII.

His statue sat in a niche on the western side, over a door to the outer church. Their focus was the huge bronze skeleton that supported the mottled marble sculpture, its arm uplifted, holding an hourglass.

It was an homage to the end of time, certainly the end of Alexander's and perhaps Bernini's as well, as he died soon after finishing it. His family had worked in the church for many years, so he could have found and hidden the stone again.

If Bernini was a Keeper, Morgan wondered, what would he have done with the precious artifact?

Two minutes until the Pope entered. They had to make a decision.

"This is it, I'm sure," Morgan whispered. "If Bernini had the stone, he would have left it here. The symbolism of the hourglass fits if he believed the stones would be together in the end times."

Jake looked up at the hourglass held by the skeletal figure of death, whatever it contained obscured by dust and time. It was also firmly attached to the skeleton's hand.

"Get ready to run. I'm going to try and break it."

A respectful hush fell over the cathedral. The choir broke into song, and all the faithful turned to the back of the basilica.

The organ pealed and the sound of a thousand cameras clicked as the Pope walked into his parish, a rock star priest amongst a flock of fans. All eyes were upon him, including those of the Swiss Guards.

Jake quickly climbed up onto the statue, wrapped a cloth around the hourglass, and smashed it with the hard edge of his phone, catching the splinters of glass in the cloth.

The choir's hymn of adoration masked the sound — but the Pope was swiftly nearing the front of the church and soon all eyes would be turned in their direction.

Jake slid back down, the wrapped fragments in his hand. "There's nothing here. It's empty. We need to go."

They ducked out of the side door under the looming skeleton.

Morgan looked up into the face of Death as she passed, a shiver of fear washing over her. Failing to find the stone put her family one step closer to that monster.

They emerged from the basilica and hurried away, out into the streets of Rome, stopping at a café to gather their thoughts.

"It was too much to hope that we would just find it there," Jake said. "But a full search of the Vatican archives is beyond our capability at this point. We may not be able to find all the stones, but we have to try for the other ones before it's too late."

Morgan held her head in her hands, eyes closed as she racked her brain, desperate to find the answer to where Peter's stone might be.

She shook her head. "I'm not giving up on this one yet. Just give me a little time."

Jake ordered them some coffee and cannoli, the sweet pastries a welcome sugar rush.

Morgan stared out the window at people passing by, wondering how she could have been so wrong, chastising herself for wasting precious time. Jake checked an email from Martin — something about Andrew and Amalfi — but Morgan still thought about Peter. If any of the stones survived, then Peter's must have been the most protected, the most precious.

Something nudged at her memory.

Something about the body of Pius — and his coat of arms.

Grabbing her phone, Morgan checked up on some facts and turned the phone so Jake could see the Pope's coat of arms. Crossed keys with a lion and an anchor.

"Look, the lion of St Mark. Pius was Patriarch of Venice before he was Pope, and the evangelist Mark supposedly accompanied Peter on his travels. One gift of the stones is communication, and Mark's Gospel became the basis of Christian orthodoxy across the world. He was like a beloved son to Peter, so it makes sense that he took the stone after the Apostle's death."

Morgan gave a triumphant smile. "The stone of St Peter must be in Venice."

CHAPTER 14

Desert outside Tucson, Arizona. May 22

JOSEPH EVERETT WATCHED THROUGH the one-way mirror as Faye tucked Gemma into the small bed in the sparsely furnished cell. He listened as she finished telling her daughter a story.

"The little girl was very brave and didn't cry, even though she was trapped in the magic castle."

Gemma curled up under the blanket. "The princess is coming to save her, isn't she, Mummy?"

"Of course, my darling, but the princess has to have adventures along the way, so she's a little late."

Gemma frowned, her tiny face screwed up with confusion. "What 'ventures?"

"Sleep time now. I'll tell you about the adventures tomorrow." Faye bent to kiss the little girl's cheek and stroke her hair, turning the desk lamp away so Gemma's face was in shadow.

Joseph leaned closer to the glass. The woman was definitely resilient, or at least hid her fear well in front of the child. When they returned after the kiln, Faye had snatched Gemma into her arms and held her tight, burying her head in the little girl's hair until the protesting child pushed her away.

After that brief loss of control, Faye smiled and pretended nothing had happened. She compartmentalized the experience and would not let her own terror affect her daughter.

Joseph raised his hand to the glass and traced the outline of Faye's face as she sat on the bed, looking down at Gemma.

He felt a sudden pang of longing for this woman and a little girl to love. Could life have been like this if his mother had been different? What if she had tucked her boys in at night and told them such stories? All he could remember were insults, pain, and the filthy cupboard under the stairs. Only Michael had told him stories in the dark, stroking his hair as Faye did for her daughter.

Could he take this woman for himself? Would she ever love him?

Joseph shook his head, wondering at his temporary weakness. Faye was nothing but a bargaining chip. Michael was his only family.

He slammed his hand against the glass.

Faye started in surprise at the sound, instinctively bending her body to protect her daughter. Gemma woke and started crying.

Joseph stalked from the hidden room, focused on the endgame. It was time to make his final plans for the day of Pentecost.

Venice, Italy. May 22.

Darkness shrouded Piazza San Marco as Morgan and Jake approached by boat, the smell of salty ocean on the light breeze.

Gondolas bobbed in the canal, gold trim glinting in the dark as water slapped against the sides in the quiet night. By day, the well-worn paths from St Mark's to L'Accademia were packed with tourists, but now only a few people walked along the banks of the lagoon.

Morgan had visited Venice for the Biennale with Elian one summer. Golden light colored her memories of the city, reflecting on the water in the city of lovers. Music filled the air as string quartets played on the streets and the mood was champagne fizz and dancing.

But the only strain of music she heard now was a

lament for lost love. She pushed the heavy thoughts away as the motorboat pulled alongside the wharf at St Mark's Square.

They hopped off the boat and headed across the piazza. Two imposing pink and grey granite columns loomed above, standing guard since the twelfth century. St Mark's winged lion gazed out to sea from the top of one, and St Theodore, the first protector of Venice, perched on the other, an ancient dragon-crocodile beneath his feet. Early Venetians executed criminals between the two pillars before baying crowds, and even now, modern city-dwellers would not walk between them in case bad luck followed through.

Legend told that the original Venetians were noblemen who fled from ancient Troy, and Morgan could see how the grandeur of days past was still aflame in the memory of this proud people. The twin columns cast shadows onto the square, reflections in the water that flowed out of drain holes. The lagoon city flooded over sixty times a year — and this was one of those nights. Morgan and Jake sloshed in rubber boots toward the basilica. It was nearly midnight, and they didn't have long to achieve their goal.

A whistle came from the shadow of the Doge's Palace, and another man joined them, his wiry frame hung with an oilskin jacket against the damp chill.

He and Jake exchanged a rough handshake, then he turned to Morgan.

"Welcome to Venice. I'm Mario, head of the ARKANE team in the city."

"Why is ARKANE working here?" Morgan asked.

"This." Mario pointed down at the floodwaters that chilled their feet. "There are many who believe Venice won't last another generation. A larger than usual flood, a tidal wave, a freak weather event, and this floating city will drown. We catalog, study — and sometimes remove — religious artworks. The great paintings of Titian and Tintoretto, and the statues of Canova, are all under threat. The two-meter flood of 1966 devastated the city, so we need to protect what is here for when the waters come again. They will come — it's just a matter of time."

He noticed Morgan shiver. "But it's cold out here. Let's get inside."

They waded through the ankle-deep water to the basilica. Even in the muted light from the street lamps, it was a kaleidoscope of multicolored marble. Each pillar supporting the church was a different kind of stone, sourced from around the world to demonstrate the glory of La Serenissima, the Venetian republic.

Stunning mosaics decorated panels above the intricately carved doors, one showing St Mark's corpse rescued from Egypt in the ninth century, smuggled to Venice under a pile of pork so Muslims wouldn't search the cargo. There was a myth that St Mark once washed up in the marshes of the Venetian lagoon after a storm and an angel told him that his body would rest here, eventually. Hundreds of years later, it came to pass.

With the help of Martin's ARKANE database, they had discovered that Pius ordered urgent repairs to the Basilica of St Mark's while he was Patriarch in 1901. He could have hidden the stone then before relocating to the Vatican.

Morgan dared hope they would find it here, her desperation increasing with the imminent threat to her family. The skeptic in her doubted the stones had any power, but the weight of history and legend was beginning to make an impression and Peter's must surely be the most important of the artifacts. The Rock of the Church, the denier who became a champion of the gospel, who died in Nero's bloody vengeance for the great fire of Rome.

Mario led them around the edge of the building and in through a side door. "The basilica was built as a mausoleum and private chapel for the Doge, the elected ruler of Venice. It's attached to his palace but we'll go in this way to avoid the cameras on that side. So what are we looking for?"

"A piece of stone," Morgan said.

Mario laughed, the sound echoing in the cavernous dark. "Have you visited the basilica before?"

"It's been years since I came for the Biennale and we didn't make it inside but… wow!"

Mario shone his powerful flashlight into the dark, illuminating patches of the walls, ceiling, and floor. "We have a lot of stone here. Over eight thousand square meters of mosaic cover the walls, vaults, and cupolas of St Mark's. Where do you want to start? Any information might help narrow it down."

Morgan gazed around at the glorious interior of the basilica, grateful for this glimpse of the holy place with no tourists to block their view of magnificence. "We're looking for a piece of rock that was part of the Pentecost story."

Mario grinned. "This is the right church for Pentecost. Come upstairs to the balcony viewing platform. Be careful now."

He handed out headlamps, which Morgan and Jake put on, keeping their hands free to help climb. The steps were ancient and worn, with enormous gaps between them that made it hard for pilgrims to mount, but easier to defend against invaders in ancient times.

They reached the viewing platform and Mario swung his powerful flashlight beam out over the abyss below, then up to the ceiling of the main dome. "That's the Pentecost mural with the Holy Spirit descending onto the twelve Apostles."

Morgan stared up at a huge circular mosaic depicting twelve seated men arrayed like a clock face. A stream of fire touched each of them, emanating from the throne of God in the center. Four angels stood with wings outstretched, bright gold encircling them all.

She used powerful binoculars to examine the mosaic, each tile a miniature masterpiece of precious metals and rare colorful stones. "There's definitely something on the throne of God, right in the center of the mosaic."

It looked like a small grey stone, its dull simplicity stark against the bright gold and rich colors around it, but it could be the real treasure of the mosaic.

Had Pius hidden the Apostle's stone in plain sight?

CHAPTER 15

Morgan passed the binoculars to Jake and turned to Mario. "How can we get a closer look?"

Mario rubbed his chin in thought. "The dome is directly over the nave, fifty meters above the ground. There's no time for scaffolding, but we have a drone used for salvage at the church of Maria Salute. That might work."

Jake nodded. "If it's our only choice, we have to try."

Mario looked at his watch. "It will be the quickest way to check if anything is up there. It's just next door in the Doge's Palace. I'll be back in fifteen minutes. Sit tight, you two. Enjoy the view."

He headed back down into the darkness of the basilica, his footsteps fading away into silence.

Now they had a moment to stop, Morgan felt the rush of the last few days catching up with her. The need for just a moment of respite was overwhelming. "Can we turn off the lights and just be in the dark for a bit? It's so peaceful here."

"Of course."

She could hear exhaustion in Jake's voice as well. The pace of this mission was taking it out of them both.

They turned off their headlamps and sat in silence, leaning back against the ancient stone. The smell of incense was strong even at night, but the stink of the overflowing sewers was a dark tone beneath, a pervasive problem of the flooding.

In the quiet, Morgan felt an affinity with Jake, the first real tendrils of partnership. She spoke into the darkness. "Wasn't there talk of a flood barrier to protect the city?"

"There have been all kinds of plans to stop the waters rising, but they've achieved little and the city still floods regularly. We may be scuba diving in this basilica in our lifetime."

Morgan imagined the eerie sensation of diving here, marble pillars looming from murky green water and the glint of gold from underwater flashlights on the intricate mosaics. "That would be amazing — but devastating."

In the darkness, Jake shifted beside her.

He was close, but not quite touching. She could

smell his clean scent and feel his body heat. Morgan wanted to lean into him, to be held for just a moment in his muscular arms. There was a connection between them, a spark of attraction that could explode with passion — or violence.

Ghosts haunted them both in the dark, chilling their skin, pulling them away from the abyss of what could be. Morgan remained rigid, unbending even as Jake spoke from the dark.

"Are you doing this with any sense of belief about the stones or just for Faye and Gemma?" His voice contained no trace of judgment, only curiosity.

Morgan felt safe, concealed in the dark. It gave her courage to speak her mind to a man she was beginning to trust. "I believe in something beyond our experience, a realm above the physical that I can't see or touch, but I sense sometimes in certain places. I don't believe in a savior who died for my sins, or a personal God who cares if I'm hurting. But I think there's an energy beyond us, a power of good and evil, a light that gives life and a darkness that can destroy. What do you think?"

Jake's voice was gentle, almost wistful. "I used to be a Christian once, but not anymore. I've seen too much over my years with ARKANE. I don't believe in what people call God, but there is something more than us out there, for sure."

Morgan was silent for a moment. The darkness was a cloak over their honesty, their first genuine conversation held in the vastness of this magical place.

"I feel closest to whatever God is when I scuba dive," she said softly. "When I sense my insignificance on the face of the earth."

She paused as memories flooded back. "Once I lay back on a dive alone and looked up through giant kelp to the surface. The sun shone down through deep green fronds, their pods waving in the surge. I saw God in that moment, in the tiny worlds living out their lives under the oceans, with no thought of us."

Jake shifted in the dark. "What of the magnificent churches we've visited over the last few days? Do you feel God here, or back in Rome or Santiago?"

Morgan ran a hand over the stone flagstones beneath her. "This is an amazing place, but the intent of this cathedral is to awe the faithful, signifying the power and riches of the Doge and the Venetian republic. I find more spirituality in nature, where humanity's hand is unseen."

"And what about the stones?" Jake asked. "Is Pentecost a myth built on a grain of truth, or a genuine power that will return if the stones are reunited? If one stone can perform miracles like Varanasi, what will all twelve do in one place?"

Morgan shrugged. "I don't believe in a power that can change matter or perform miracles through pieces of rock. I'm a psychologist, and mass hysteria could explain what happened in India. Even if there were miracles, that doesn't make them from God and it doesn't matter, anyway. I need to do this to save my family. Can I count on you to help me to the end?"

Jake's silence was just a fraction too long, but then they heard the door creak open below and footsteps echoed through the church as Mario returned.

Morgan and Jake switched their headlamps back on and blinked a little in the light. They avoided each other's eyes. It was as if the honest conversation in the dark had never happened.

Mario reappeared on the balcony, struggling with a metal suitcase. He put it down and opened it to reveal a drone with pincers, a tiny drill, and a mesh catch bag. "We use the attachments to plug holes and the catch bag to stop the mortar falling at Maria Salute, but I think it'll do the trick. We need to hurry, though. It's pretty loud and we can't get caught here. I'm not sure even Director Marietti could placate the Patriarch of Venice over the desecration of the Basilica."

Fitting the equipment together, Mario and Jake made sure the rotors spun properly and started it up. The loud buzzing echoed around the dome.

While Jake spotlighted the stone with a stronger hand-held beam, Mario used the controls to hover the drone above the ledge and then directed it up to the Pentecost cupola. "There's a mini camera on the drill. Check out the image on the monitor."

Morgan knelt by the tiny screen, her anticipation building at the sight of their goal. "It's a grainy image, but the center stone is clearly different from the other mosaic tiles. That must be it."

Mario expertly maneuvered the drone as he drilled around the side of the stone, neatly positioning the catch bag underneath to catch the debris. "Almost there. I just have to lever it out… Okay, it's in the bag."

He guided the drone back to the balcony and shut it down.

Jake opened the catch bag, sifted through the fragments, and scooped out the stone. One side was blank, almost worn, but the other was roughly carved with a circle within a square.

Mario looked disappointed at its humble appearance. "Is that it?"

Jake turned it over in his hand and looked at Morgan. "What do you think?"

Morgan bent to examine it more closely. "It looks like the same rock as the others, and it has to be the right one. Why else would such a piece be mounted in the center of the Pentecost mural? It must have tremendous significance."

Mario carefully packed the drone back into its case, and the trio retraced their steps down the stairs of the basilica, exiting through a hidden doorway into the Doge's Palace behind enormous marble pillars of rose and teal.

They wound their way through a maze of grand rooms with ornate paintings, chandeliers, and exquisite furniture. Mario turned into one room and led them over to a corner where the wallpaper showed the outline of a door beneath.

"Behind here lies the authentic Venice, the real halls of power where the secrets of the Republic lay hidden. There are prison cells, even a torture chamber. Casanova was imprisoned here. He was one of the few who escaped."

Morgan shivered, memories of what she once suffered at the hands of those in power invading her thoughts. "Governments are all the same throughout the ages. Nothing changes."

Mario shook his head. "Not always true. Venice was one of the most impressive early democracies. The government had a complicated election process that prevented the nepotism and despotism that plagued other parts of Europe back then — and indeed affect many now. It was truly a light in the medieval darkness of tyranny on the Continent."

Morgan heard pride in his voice and defense of his beloved city. She had similar conflicting feelings about Jerusalem, a city she both loved and despised, where truth was ever malleable and people's lives hung in the balance of the great religions. Perhaps Venice was just as complicated.

Mario led them through the maze of narrow wooden corridors and through tiny rooms with low ceilings, half the height of the grand rooms below, so two levels could fit into each. Tiny windows lay camouflaged in the walls outside, providing little light in the dark space. The civil servants of the Venetian government once toiled away here, the true power behind La Serenissima.

They finally reached a large open-plan document room with wooden panels painted with coats of arms representing the noble families who ruled Venice for generations.

Morgan sank down into a chair, the stone tucked deep into her inside jacket pocket, close to her heart. She wasn't letting it go. Even after their honest conversation in the dark of the basilica, she didn't trust Jake's motives for seeking the stones.

Mario pulled out some blankets from a cupboard. "You can rest here for a few hours, as long as you leave before the workers come in. Venetians are late starters, though. They like to have their coffee first."

Morgan nodded, barely able to keep her eyes open. She made a rough bed with some blankets and curled up, grateful for her ability to sleep quickly, even under great stress, a skill she'd picked up in the Israeli military. She closed her eyes and let the world sink away.

Jake stood in front of a bay window at the opposite end of the room. He called Marietti and whispered so as not to wake Morgan.

"We have the stone of St Peter. Morgan was right. It was here in Venice."

"Excellent. It's imperative that you also get the others before Thanatos finds you again."

Jake frowned. "We've had no trouble here. Maybe they've lost our trail."

"Or maybe they've gone after other stones. Since you're in Italy, Martin's research indicates you should head to Amalfi next, for the relics of St Andrew. There's evidence they were taken there after the Sack of Constantinople. We'll speak again after that."

Marietti ended the call and Jake stared out the window at the dark lagoon lapping against the side of the Doge's Palace. The lights on the Ponte della Paglia illuminated the ancient dungeons connected to the palace by the Bridge of Sighs, named after the sighs of the damned.

As Jake turned to look at Morgan's sleeping form, he felt as if he walked among those ghosts of ancient Venice, trapped into reliving their bleak sentence every night.

CHAPTER 16

Salerno to Amalfi, Italy. May 23

MORGAN STARED OUT ACROSS the azure ocean as the speedboat bumped across the waves, the wind in her hair and the sun on her face a welcome refreshment. They had risen early in Venice and flown to Salerno, where they hired a skipper with a boat to take them around the coast to their next destination.

Amalfi was on the opposite coast of Italy from Venice, nestled at the bottom of the dramatic cliffs of Monte Cerreto, on the edge of the Gulf of Salerno to the southeast of Naples. A center of medieval power around the turn of the first millennium, its natural harbor made it a popular holiday spot for the British aristocracy in the 1920s. Now tourists visited mainly for the gorgeous coastline and the limoncello, pressed from lemons on the hilly slopes above.

Morgan looked back on the last few days as a blur — running, hiding, creeping around in the darkness, and desecrating churches. It was a relief to be out in the sunlight, the rich colors something she missed in the grey of England. Israel had this quality of light too, with the brilliant blue of its sky rarely seen in Oxford.

She closed her eyes behind dark sunglasses and lifted her face to the sun, wishing they had time to swim in the bright ocean.

Memories of a day trip with Faye and Gemma flooded back. Brighton beach on a surprisingly sunny day in April. Deckchairs set out on a stony shore while seagulls swooped low to snatch discarded fish and chips. Ice cream sellers hawked sugary treats to the British holiday-makers soaking up the much-needed rays. Knowing the vagaries of the weather forecast, the sisters had taken sweaters and waterproofs as well as bathing suits and towels and made a nest on the beach.

While Faye relaxed with a book, Morgan took Gemma's hand and led her down to the ocean. The little girl's face was a rapture of delight as gentle waves tickled her feet and they splashed together in the shallows. Gemma giggled and squealed at the cold as they darted in and out. Simple pleasures with her family. Morgan blinked away tears, grateful for her dark glasses.

Jake interrupted her thoughts as he sat down beside her, holding his phone with more information from Martin back at ARKANE. "St Andrew certainly got around. Did you know he's the patron saint of Ukraine, Scotland, Russia, Romania, and Greece, as well as here in Amalfi, and other cities in Portugal and Malta?"

Morgan gazed out at the view. "So why does Martin think the stone is here?"

"The cathedral of Amalfi is dedicated to him. After the sack of Constantinople, the Apostle's relics were transported there in 1208, although Andrew's head only joined the rest of his body eight hundred years later. If the Keepers followed the bones of the Apostles, there must be something here."

They disembarked at the Porto di Amalfi next to the mega yachts and other luxury craft in the wide bay. Towering cliffs, unchanged for millennia, overshadowed white houses with red roofs interspersed with green olive groves. Terraced hillsides stretched above them, with glimpses of hidden palazzos and boutique villas nestled into the headland.

Morgan and Jake headed out of the marina and pushed through the hordes of tourists who thronged the marina walls. The hotels on the waterfront were brilliant white, with racing-green shutters. The largest buildings had buttresses and towers climbing uphill; the town could only grow upward here as the cliffs pushed it into the sea. There were old-style iron lamp posts and iconic Vespa scooters parked on the street.

Morgan smiled. "This is such a different Italy. I'd love to stay awhile. I know Faye would love it here, too." She thought of Faye's amazing cooking, so different from her own functional relationship with food. Her sister's *melanzane alla Parmigiana* could definitely hold its own even in this Italian heartland.

"Hold that thought," Jake replied. "You'll be able to come back with Faye. I know you will."

They entered the pedestrian section of the town and walked up narrow streets, past tourist shops and cafés to reach the cathedral square with its ancient bell tower. Cafés and *pasticcerie* dotted the plaza, with red tablecloths and carafes of wine on tables, while happy tourists basked in the sun.

Morgan sneaked a glance at couples holding hands and felt a twinge of jealousy, a pang of longing. Happiness was fleeting in this world, but its ephemeral nature made it all the more precious.

The cathedral had a black-and-white facade, striped and decorated with arched lattice windows reminiscent of the Mezquita at Cordoba in Spain, an amalgamation of Jewish, Muslim, and Christian decoration. A long, wide staircase led up to the front entrance of the cathedral with shops tucked underneath, every spare inch a business opportunity.

A motorbike engine roared suddenly.

Shouts rang out from the church.

A denim-clad rider on a bright red sports bike sped out of the cathedral and down the steps.

Tourists screamed and threw themselves out of the way as the rider bumped his way down. He shot off the last step, skidded a little, and raced off into the labyrinth of the Amalfi passageways.

"Thanatos," Jake shouted. "It has to be." He ran to a parked scooter at the side of the square.

Morgan saw her chance and nudged a passing tourist off a Vespa as he stood idling in the erupting chaos. She jumped on and accelerated after the speeding bike, leaving the rider in the dust.

She raced after the biker, senses heightened as she plunged into the narrow streets.

Screams and angry shouts came from ahead as tourists bottle-necked the streets. She must be gaining on him.

The streets were narrow, with tall buildings several floors high and stone archways joining them over the top. The Vespa struggled on the steepest parts but Morgan glimpsed the biker's denim jacket through the crowds.

She pushed through faster, revving the little Vespa to clear the way in front of her.

He would make a mistake at some point, then she'd be on him.

The biker headed away from the main tourist track into the back streets of Amalfi, overlooked by cast-iron streetlights and balconies with mini palms, with looming mountains behind. The walls were still Mediterranean-white but stained with graffiti further away from the tourist hub.

The wind whipped some hanging laundry in front of Morgan and she thrust it away as she turned another corner. She hadn't been on a motorbike for a few years now, but she'd ridden with Elian in the desert, even street racing in Tel Aviv. As she zoomed along, she realized she missed the adrenalin rush of the chase. It seemed she couldn't entirely bury her old self with academia.

Morgan turned a corner and into a dead end. The biker clearly wasn't a local either, and they were both lost.

He turned his bike and revved it as he prepared to come back at her — gun in hand.

Morgan braked and sheltered by the corner of a wall. The biker didn't have a clear shot yet, but he would as soon as he accelerated out of the dead end.

She raced her engine — and gunned out as he tried to pass in front of her.

Bracing for impact, Morgan crashed straight into the side of his bike and knocked him into a wall. He lay trapped under the heavy machine, gun ripped from his hand.

Morgan jumped off her scooter, grabbed his gun, and pointed it down at him.

She flipped the safety off and held the gun under his chin, speaking slowly but firmly as she pressed the muzzle down hard. "Give me the stone."

"There's no stone. I couldn't find it." He spoke English with a rough Italian accent. "I have nothing. Get off me!"

Morgan's voice was low and calm, the threat apparent. "I don't believe you. Where is it?"

Sirens echoed through the streets as the carabinieri drew closer.

Jake sped around the corner on his scooter, skidding to a halt nearby. "We don't have much time, Morgan. Does he have it?"

She glared round, gun still held against the biker's chin. "Back off, Timber. This one's mine."

Jake backed away at the possession in her voice, a predator defending her kill.

Morgan moved the barrel of the gun to the man's exposed knee, thrust forward by his position half under the bike. "I need that stone."

He sneered at her. "You don't have time for this."

Without so much as a change in expression, Morgan shot point blank into his knee.

The biker howled in agony as he clutched at the shattered bone, the pale horse tattoo clear on his forearm. Blood dripped down onto the pristine paint of the motorcycle.

Jake rushed forward, but Morgan swung the gun at him. "I mean it, Jake."

He put his hands up in surrender and retreated.

Morgan bent low and put the gun against the biker's crotch. "One more time. Where's the stone?"

"*Puttana*," he spat. "If you take it, they'll kill me."

He was pleading now, but his hand moved to his chest.

Keeping the gun on him, Morgan pulled the zip of his jacket down and reached in for the stone. She pulled it out in a white handkerchief, a surge of triumph washing over her.

The sound of running feet came from the alleys beyond as the carabinieri closed in on their position.

Morgan and Jake climbed the wall at the dead end of the street and ran back down the hill to the marina. Exhausted, they dropped into the boat and the skipper cast off, heading back over the waves.

Back at Salerno, Morgan and Jake boarded the plane, having hardly said a word on the journey.

Morgan's actions sat between them, uncomfortably acknowledged but not discussed. She had crossed a line by turning the gun on Jake, but a haze of anger overwhelmed her in the moment. The biker embodied everything that threatened Faye and Gemma, and she'd wanted to hurt him — badly.

She had tried to leave that side of her behind in Israel. Violence only spiraled into more violence, as the country's own bitter history demonstrated. But were such actions justified for the end result? After all, they had the next stone.

Jake sat across from her, reading quietly as they considered the next destination. Morgan understood that neither of them were team players and she had pushed his help away back in Amalfi. The tentative relationship that sprouted in the Venice night had been torn apart by her actions. She felt the need to reach out to Jake, to patch up what was unsaid and unacknowledged. This was no time for division.

Morgan leaned forward. "We don't have the stone of Philip yet. He was the most organized of the Apostles, the steward of the group." She pointed at the notes from Father Ben.

"He preached in Ethiopia and North Africa, but

died in Jerusalem — either of old age or perhaps beheaded as a martyr. The Church suppressed his gospel as heresy, as it portrayed the more esoteric side of Jesus's teaching. Helena, the mother of Constantine, took his relics to Germany. They're held in the Abbey Church of Trier, built in the twelfth century but still an active monastery."

"So the stone could be in Trier?" Jake said.

Morgan shrugged. "Perhaps, but there's no evidence of miracles there and Philip was mostly active in Jerusalem. I think we have to go to Israel."

Jake looked incredulous. "Jerusalem is packed with relics and religious artifacts. Plus, it's a security nightmare. How can we possibly find the Keeper or the stone in such a short timeframe?"

Morgan sat back. "I know Jerusalem, so I can navigate our path, and it might not be as difficult as you think. Philip preached to the Ethiopians for much of his career and wrote his gospel there. The Ethiopian Coptic church is one of the most ancient and is even rumored to protect the Ark of the Covenant."

Jake raised an eyebrow. "Like Indiana Jones?"

Morgan laughed. "There's a legend that the Ark was taken to Ethiopia by Menelik, son of Solomon and the Queen of Sheba. Whatever the truth, the Ethiopian Coptics are certainly good at keeping ancient secrets. It makes sense that if there were a Keeper for Philip's stone, they would know who it might be. All we have to do is persuade them to help us."

BREAKING NEWS

BBC News, May 24: Comet not seen since the time of Christ crosses Earth's orbit.

THE RESURGAM COMET WILL light up the night sky during the next week as the body of celestial matter crosses Earth's orbit, streaming a colored tail of dust and gas.

The comet was named with the Latin *resurgam*, meaning 'I shall rise again' since it hasn't been seen since 33 AD, the time of Jesus Christ. In ancient times, comets were bad omens and, indeed, some have claimed that the violent weather events currently wreaking havoc across the world are related to the comet's approach.

Celestial influence was identified recently with Elenin, a comet that passed by in 2011. During the period it aligned with the Earth and the Sun, earthquakes were felt in Japan, New Zealand, and Chile.

Scientists are concerned that the Resurgam comet might have a similar impact, bringing widespread natural disturbances. Conspiracy theorists claim the government is covering up the possibility of cataclysmic events, but repeated statements downplay the potential impact.

Religious groups claim the comet underpins biblical references to the end times. Pastor Jesse Warren of San Bernardino said, "The gospel of St Mark says that in the end times there will be earthquakes and famines. The Earth will darken, and the moon will not give its light. The stars will fall from the sky, and the heavenly bodies will be shaken. These are the beginnings of birth-pains, for the new world will be born in this turmoil."

The best views of the comet will be in desert areas of the Northern Hemisphere, away from city lights. Sightings can be logged on the NASA website, which will track the comet's movement across the skies.

CHAPTER 17

MORGAN AND JAKE ENTERED the courtyard in front of the Church of the Holy Sepulchre, an ancient building crushed into the dense heart of the Old City. It nestled within the walls of the souk, huddled amongst market stalls brimming with religious trinkets and street food stalls piled high with local delights.

Tourists wandered around eating felafel and sweet harissa cakes, exchanging shekels for Palestinian glass, Jerusalem T-shirts, and statues of the Virgin Mary. Perhaps it was appropriate, for Jesus ministered to the merchants, the sinners, the real people of this city.

Morgan felt a bittersweet joy at walking these streets again. She reveled in the sun on her skin while the smells of the souk permeated the air around them. Despite its conflict, Jerusalem was her home and England would never arouse this passion in her.

But there were ghosts here, too.

Elian smiled from a doorway of a teahouse. Her father bent over a manuscript in an antique bookseller's shop.

This country had dashed her heart on its ancient rocks. It thrived on a fast-moving river of bloodshed and violence, and Morgan had been sinking into its depths. She left to save herself, but as sunlight dappled the cobblestones of the Old City, she had a moment of regret. Her relationship with the city of God wasn't over yet, but this trip could only be a fleeting visit. There was no time to rekindle her love for the place.

Morgan weaved between the noisy tourist groups and led Jake to the entrance of the Holy Sepulchre, the most sacred church in the Christian world. It was a short walk from the Western Wall, the only part of the Jewish Temple left standing and holy to Jews. The Temple Mount stood behind, topped by the golden Dome of the Rock shrine sacred to Muslims. This ancient city was the heart of three great religions and yet, it wasn't far to the shopping malls of Ben Yehuda Street, the high-tech startups of Tel Aviv, or the advanced military installations dotted around the country. Israel sheltered both the truly ancient and seriously modern within its contested borders.

Tour groups of different nationalities thronged the small square in front of the Holy Sepulchre, following guides who held umbrellas high and shouted to be heard.

This was Christianity Grand Central, as millions of faithful arrived on pilgrimage each year. Morgan led the way through the crowd, glancing back now and then to make sure Jake was still close.

They entered the church in a haze of incense, a cloying sensory overload. Morgan coughed in the dense atmosphere, comparing it to the airy synagogue her father once worshipped in. She wondered how Christians could stand the smell, for it made her feel heady and nauseous.

They squeezed past the Stone of Anointing, hung with ornate candleholders like canopic jars suspended over praying pilgrims. A ray of sunlight lanced in from the entrance, but most of the interior was lit only by strings of lamps and candles with flickering flames.

The faithful pushed and shoved their way forward in the loud and unbearably hot church. Sticky hands pawed at locations of torture and death, cameras flashed, while pickpockets prowled the crowds, finding easy pickings from the rich Westerners who flocked from America and Europe on pilgrimage.

At Calvary, more candles illuminated the faces of gathered believers lost in prayer, even as those behind jostled for a place. Pilgrims queued to put their hands down a golden-rimmed portal to touch the rock where Christ was crucified, some kneeling to kiss the ground. Icons and paintings on the walls added to the atmosphere with bloody images of the scourging and crucifixion of Jesus, depicted in horrific detail.

Morgan walked on through the crowd until they reached the center of the church, where Christian denominations jostled uncomfortably together. It was a highly political building, a mishmash of theology and architecture composed of Roman Catholics, Eastern Orthodox, the breakaway Armenian church, and the Ethiopian Coptics. United in believing that Jesus died and rose again, these groups still debated most other aspects of faith after thousands of years. Grievances between the groups still caused physical blows in the one of the holiest places in Christendom.

A first-century shrine lay next to the Syrian chapel in the east end of the church, behind the Holy Sepulchre.

Morgan pointed at the entrance. "This isn't even the real tomb of Jesus. Helena, mother of the

Emperor Constantine, decided it would be here in 300 AD. After all, Jesus wasn't famous when he died. Just another criminal to the Romans, another failed Messianic pretender to the Jews, so they did not mark the place on any map."

"How do you know it's wrong?" Jake asked.

"It's inside the walled city for a start, and the Romans crucified people *outside* the gates, leaving the unclean bodies to rot on the crosses. The most likely place for Golgotha is actually the main bus station in Jerusalem."

Jake raised an eyebrow. "Seriously? That's hardly appropriate for the spiritual center of the Church."

"I don't know." Morgan gestured at the crowds. "This is a chaotic place. Perhaps a dirty bus terminal is more fitting as a transit center for the crossroads of humanity. If you look up to the white cliffs above the station, you can still see holes in the rock walls. The 'place of the skull' eroded and chiseled away by two thousand years of weathering."

She paused for a moment, thinking of more peaceful times. "There's a place outside the walls, a garden that some believe is Gethsemane, where Jesus spent his last night crying out to God. The olive trees are thousands of years old and it's still a place of meditation and quiet prayer. There's even a rock-hewn tomb that might have been owned by Nicodemus, the priest."

"You sound like you almost believe it," Jake said.

Morgan shrugged. "Does it matter where the real place lies? Faith is in the heart."

Jake stared out over the crowds of people. "So many nationalities, so many unique expressions of faith. Jerusalem is like a religious theme park with experience junkies snapping pictures and loading up with tacky icons. But I can't see anything related to Pentecost here. At least, it's not obvious like the basilica in Venice."

Morgan nodded. "You're right. The story of Pentecost isn't strong here. It's celebrated as part of the ecclesiastical calendar, but this place is all about Christ's death and resurrection, not the Acts of the Apostles that came after. But I'm sure there's at least a clue here. We just need to ask the right questions."

The Chapel of the Holy Sepulchre, where Jesus supposedly rose from the dead, was only big enough for a few people, so a long line of pilgrims curled around it. A tiny, modest Coptic chapel hid further back, ignored by the praying hordes, just big enough for a single monk to maintain constant vigilance and prayer.

They weaved through the crowds and Morgan entered into the Coptic sanctuary alone.

A monk sat in black robes with his Bible open, staring at it in meditative silence. He didn't look up as she entered. Perhaps he was weary of being a curiosity to the pilgrim-tourists who had been a daily presence for hundreds of years.

Morgan knelt by the altar, almost at the monk's feet, because the chapel was so small. "Abba," she said, using the term of respect for a father of the church.

He looked at her, a question in his eyes.

Reaching into her pocket, Morgan brought out the plain, rough-hewn stone of St James and held it before him.

He gasped and spoke swiftly in Ge'ez, an ancient Ethiopian language, pointed to the door, and motioned upward.

Morgan tried to make sense of it. "I need to speak to the head of the Coptics. Is that possible?"

He pointed again, seeming to indicate that he could not leave his post but encouraging her to speak with his people.

The stone must be here.

Back outside, Jake stared at the lines of pilgrims, a kaleidoscope of international faith.

Morgan pulled him away. "The monk definitely recognized the stone. Let's get out of here and into the fresh air."

They found the way up to the roof from the courtyard of the Greek Orthodox Patriarchate, and climbed the rough-hewn stone steps to the home of the Ethiopian Coptic Church in Jerusalem, an incongruous village of monastic cells known as Deir Al-Sultan. A strong faith sustained the tiny community despite poor conditions and meager resources.

Huts with low doorways nestled above the chapel of St Helena, one of the oldest parts of the church, where the Coptic monks and a few nuns kept their stake alive in this holy place, as close as they could get to the heart of Christendom.

An old nun sat on a metal chair in a patch of sunlight. She leaned against the side of one of the rotund shrines, her face turned to catch a few rays. Simple pleasures were to be relished even this close to God.

On their approach, she pointed above and behind, clearly accustomed to directing pilgrims for prayer or holy tourism.

Morgan and Jake walked up some rickety stairs, badly in need of repair, to the Coptic chapel of the Archangel Michael. The Ethiopian Church, although ancient, had never been wealthy like the Roman Catholics. But although this chapel was humble, it was rich in color. The bright red of the Patriarch's chair stood out against the deep mahogany of the lattice of the holy screen, and the walls were covered with vivid paintings from the story of Solomon and Sheba, central to the Ethiopian Coptic traditions. The chapel achieved a more celebratory atmosphere than the Sepulchre below, with its bloody images of suffering and sacrifice.

Fresh air blew through the chapel, a welcome break from the incense overload downstairs. A monk knelt by the altar, a vital middle-aged man, ebony skin highlighted by his bright saffron robes.

He rose to greet them with a smile of welcome. "We're closed for private prayer, but can I help you with anything?" His voice was deep and sonorous, a touch of an accent in his clearly educated English.

Morgan pulled out the stone of James. "We're looking for a piece similar to this. It belonged to the Apostle Philip and we think the Ethiopian Church might have it."

The monk reached behind them and closed the doors to the chapel, locking them in place. He ushered them further in toward the altar.

"There have been rumors that the time has come for the stones to be revealed once more. I've heard from my brothers of deaths among the Keepers, and now you are here."

His eyes betrayed his suspicions.

"There have been deaths, though not at our hands," Morgan explained. "But there are men coming who want the stones and will kill for them. If we take yours, we can lead them away from your community."

The monk sat down. "Why should I trust you?"

Morgan opened her shirt at the neck to reveal her own stone. "I'm a fellow Keeper."

He sighed, his body sagging as tension left him. "Monks have passed our stone down for generations. It was brought back here a few hundred years ago, and remained in this shrine ever since. But if you take it now, we will lose our last artifact of the Apostle."

Morgan leaned toward him, her voice gentle. "But if we don't take it now, it may be stolen by force and some of your people may be hurt. I promise that we'll protect yours with the others."

As she spoke the words, Morgan felt a twinge of unease. Her promise rang false as she planned to give the stones to Everett, but part of her believed she could still find a way to save her family — and prevent the sacred talismans from being used for evil.

The monk gazed at her, and Morgan wondered if he could discern her true motivation.

A moment passed, then he nodded. "There was a prophecy passed down with the stone. In the end times the twelve will be together again, as they were at Pentecost. Perhaps it is fitting that you take it now. There has been enough violence in this holy place. Besides, my faith is in the unseen and I live by the power of the resurrection. God does not need rocks to perform miracles."

He rose and went to the altar behind the lattice as patterns of the sun through the skylight formed a shining nimbus around him. The monk pulled out a tiny leather satchel from beneath the altar and handed it to Morgan.

"This is the stone of Philip. I give it to you as a fellow Keeper. Protect it and go with God."

Morgan took it with reverence and they left him standing there in the ancient Coptic church, a proud religion in the heart of sacred Jerusalem.

As they walked away through the winding streets of the Old City, Morgan turned to Jake. "I'm torn. These stones have been entrusted to me as a Keeper to protect and keep safe. But I have to give them up to save Faye and Gemma in only a few days' time. How can I do both?"

Jake looked down at her, his eyes shaded by the dark sunglasses he wore against the bright sun. "Maybe the choice will be made for you."

CHAPTER 18

Tel Aviv, Israel. May 24

BACK ON THE PLANE, Morgan sat with a laptop exploring the ARKANE databases, hunting for myths of Simon the Zealot, the last Apostle who held a Pentecost stone. Jake tapped away on his phone, following other possible clues.

They couldn't leave Tel Aviv until they knew the next destination — and time was running out to find the final stone before Pentecost.

Morgan found herself absorbed in secrets suppressed for millennia and realized that she could easily lose herself in this esoteric labyrinth of learning. Martin Klein had created algorithms to tag manuscripts and myths with keywords for easier relational searches, enhanced by artificial intelligence and machine learning. The data formed a vast map of different traditions, tracking ideas, artifacts, and people of history across the world.

As she tried to make sense of it all, Morgan sat back in her chair. She rubbed the base of her neck and rolled her shoulders as she called Jake over.

"Look at this map. Simon went everywhere. West from Egypt across North Africa to Carthage, then on to Britain before heading back East, where he was martyred in Persia by being sawn in half. One of his arms ended up as a relic in Cologne, Germany, but there are potential sites for the rest of his body parts as far away as Iran. Where do we even start?"

Jake leaned over to look at the details. "We left this one until last because we knew it would be the most difficult. Just try to narrow down the options."

Morgan jumped up and paced the length of the cabin. "We don't have time to sit around thinking. I need another perspective. Ben might be able to help. He's a walking encyclopedia of the early Church, so he might shed some new light on the options."

She sat back down at her laptop and called Ben. He answered quickly, his expression delighted at first but swiftly creasing into a frown. "Morgan, where are you? I've been so worried. The police are still investigating the murders here, calling them a terrorist attack on a religious institution. I've kept your name out of it so far, but Thanatos must still be after you."

Morgan smiled with reassurance. "I'm fine.

Really. It's been a whirlwind few days. We've found several more stones, but we only have a few days left. I need information on Simon the Zealot and anything you can find on his relics — and I need it as fast as possible."

Ben nodded. "I understand the haste. You must be desperately worried about Faye and Gemma. I'll head to the library now. There is knowledge here that even ARKANE doesn't know about. I'll get back to you as soon as I can."

Blackfriars, Oxford, England.

Ben logged off and gazed out of his window down into the quad. The authorities were at a loss to understand what had happened here just a few days ago. Ben played the 'forgetful old monk' card during his interviews with the police, and they bought it, assuming him to be an innocent bystander caught in the cross-fire.

No one else had seen Morgan, so her name was kept out of the news. Maybe he had Marietti to thank for that. Ben frowned. He couldn't let issues of the past prevent Morgan from saving Faye and little Gemma, but he was deeply suspicious of

ARKANE's motives, and worried about how far Thanatos might go to retrieve the stones. ARKANE dabbled at the edge of the supernatural, where shadows blurred between black and white — but sometimes they strayed too far into the grey.

Ben had several tutorials lined up that day with bright students, all eager to study Church history, and find a way for the future of faith in these dark times. He sighed. The same arguments raged now as they did millennia ago, and these new students would debate the meaning of the Trinity, the paradox of suffering, and the coming end times just as generations had before. There was nothing new under the sun, as the book of Ecclesiastes taught so well, but Ben continued to live for the joy of working here. Blackfriars was his home, where he could immerse himself in learning and teaching — and he would use its resources now to help Morgan on her quest.

Ben headed down to the Blackfriars library and sat at one of the solid wooden desks so characteristic of ascetic Oxford. The chairs were hard enough to make students want to get up and leave, but by choosing to endure physical pain, they could enrich their minds, a monastic attitude honed from centuries of belief.

The windows of the library looked out onto St Giles, a busy road in the heart of the city with leafy green trees and students riding by on bikes piled high with books. The libraries in Oxford still lent physical copies even while the contents of the Bodleian Library were being digitized. It seemed technology hadn't yet killed the desire to physically handle these old tomes.

The university was changing, albeit slowly in a fast-paced society, and Ben knew the outside world wondered why the monks made the choices they did. But he loved the simple life of contemplation and the pursuit of knowledge without the trappings of secular life. He had given that up as penance and service to the Order. His only other obligation was the protection of the twins, Morgan and Faye, his promise to their mother, Marianne, as she lay dying. This promise now drove him to the library, hoping he could find something to help.

Ben spent so much time in the library that he retained almost photographic memories of which book held what information and where each was in this cavernous space.

Ornamental stained-glass panels in the windows allowed colorful light to filter through, lighting the books in shades of vermilion and aquamarine. Each panel depicted the heraldic emblem of an important friar in the history of the Blackfriars back to the fourteenth century.

Ben pulled down the *Legenda aurea*, *The Golden Legend*, a collection of the lives of saints compiled in the thirteenth century. The oversized volume was one of many that were chained in place to stop students removing or damaging them, and had to be read standing up at a special lectern.

It was a popular ecclesiastical book and one of the first to be published by William Caxton in the English language. The original gospels, both those in the Christian Bible and those considered heretical, contained little information about the Apostles and other early Christians. But stories and traditions were passed down and collated in the *Legend*, the first popular hagiography, based on the Dominicans' own books on the lives of the saints, apocryphal texts like the Gospel of Nicodemus, and other histories. It contained visions and supernatural occurrences, myth and allegory — but beneath it all was a narrative of the travels of the Apostles.

A good place to start in the search for the stone of Simon the Zealot.

After preaching in Egypt, Simon traveled to Armenia and Persia with St Jude, also called Thaddeus. They converted many people and were both eventually martyred in Persia. In other texts, Ben found that Simon's relics were scattered all over the Christian empire, from St Peter's Basilica in the Vatican to Toulouse in France.

There was little to add to what Morgan had already discovered, so he needed to dig deeper. It was time to call in some favors from the Collegium Angelicum in Rome.

Returning to his room, Ben put in a call to the Grand Master of the Order, an old friend he studied with many years ago.

As he described what he sought, the Grand Master became wary. "Be careful, Ben. These are dangerous times to meddle with stones of power. Why are you helping this woman, and why is ARKANE involved?"

Ben sighed. "I'm not clear on ARKANE's motives, but Morgan and her sister Faye are like daughters to me. I vowed to protect them — a sacred promise made to a dying friend whose secrets I keep to this day."

The Grand Master wheezed as he spoke, the hardship of advanced age in his voice. "If you are determined on this course, then I speak off the record as an old friend, not as your Grand Master. The stones first came to our notice when Nazi relic hunters visited the Vatican asking questions during the Second World War. They followed myths to locate supernatural weapons, and while we sent them away with nothing, it encouraged the Order to look into the Pentecost stones with more interest.

I believe they even found some before the world order shifted once more — but you know all about that time."

Ben's voice was heavy with regret. "Yes, it seems those old enemies may be rising again. I have seen the pale horse of Thanatos myself."

"Then you must take great care, for these old ghosts are hungry for blood."

Ben walked back and forth in his office. "I didn't seek this fight. It has come to my door and threatens those I promised to protect. I must do this. What can you tell me about the stone of Simon the Zealot?"

The Grand Master was silent for a moment and the rustling of papers came over the line before he spoke once more. "A family in Egypt kept it safe, but over time, the Keepers were corrupted, their faith eroded by the spread of militant Islam. They sold the stone onto the antiquities market in the early 1900s and it's rumored that the psychologist Carl Jung bought it when he was in Tunis in 1920. He collected curiosities related to religious myth, and the story fascinated him. We lost track of it after that — but perhaps you should follow the trail of Carl Jung into the deserts of North Africa."

Tel Aviv, Israel. May 24.

Morgan listened to the story, fascinated by the possible history of Simon the Zealot's stone. Ben was on speakerphone, with Martin Klein connected from the ARKANE headquarters, hoping that between them they could narrow down locations.

"The psychologist Carl Jung traveled to the oasis of Nefta while he was in Tunisia in 1920," Ben said. "His memoirs note that he felt an alien sense of being European in a Moorish desert land, soaked with the blood of Carthage, Rome, and later the Christians. Evidently, it was a powerful experience, and he recounted a dream of a citadel in the desert, where he fought with and then taught a royal Arab his secrets. Morgan, you've studied Jung's writings in depth. Did he ever mention a Pentecost stone?"

Morgan frowned as she recalled her studies of Jung. "I don't remember Pentecost mentioned specifically, but Jung was certainly fascinated with stone. He carved rocks with sacred words and images as part of his creative retreats, and some still lie at his tower in Bollingen on Lake Zurich in Switzerland. If the trip was so personal, perhaps there's something in The Red Book?"

Jake held up a hand to stop her. "What's The Red Book and why is it so important?"

Morgan explained. "It was Jung's journal, written during a breakdown between 1913 and 1929. It's an oversized red leather-bound book with writing and paintings about his thoughts, visions, and dreams. Jung believed that ancient myths still resonate in the modern world through the collective unconscious. He even dreamt about rivers of blood drowning Europe in the years before the Second World War."

Martin jumped in, his voice crackling over the line. "Many of the paintings in The Red Book are representations of mandala, a circle in a square representing the inward journey of the soul. It also contains images from Egyptian myth, particularly snakes, representing renewal and creation, as well as the Deceiver. The snake is a powerful symbol in many—"

Jake cut off his enthusiastic oratory. "Thanks, Martin, that's enough for now. Can you send images, please?"

"Of course, I'll send them now. I've seen the real thing, Morgan. It's amazing! I was one of the few present when The Red Book came out of the Swiss vault to be photographed. The family kept it pristine for years, with hardly a soul looking at it, so the colors are still fresh."

As they waited for Martin to email the images, Morgan considered his exclusive access to The Red

Book. She had an oversized full-color reproduction, but Martin's unique experience piqued her professional jealousy. Working for ARKANE certainly had its benefits.

The images arrived, and they opened the first file.

Jake leaned in closer. "Is that what I think it is?"

The image showed a square room with turquoise-patterned walls and a red-and-black checkered floor. A man knelt in worship, his head on the ground, his arms reaching toward a small grey stone. A pillar of fire and flame rose from it, filling the room with sparks and smoke, billowing above the man as if about to consume him.

Martin's voice crackled on the line again. "I've pulled satellite images of the desert around Nefta, where Jung visited an oasis. There's an ancient citadel near the wadi constructed like a mandala, a circle within a square. It can't be a coincidence."

Morgan looked over at Jake, her hopes colliding with doubt. "We only have time for one more journey before Pentecost, but we don't have any better options at this point. We have to try."

"You'll need backup for the citadel," Martin said. "It's currently used as a training facility for a local extremist group."

Jake sighed. "Thanks, Martin. See if you can mobilize Jared Rush's team out of Egypt. They should be able to get there about the same time as us."

As the plane took off soon after, Morgan closed her eyes and willed herself to Faye and Gemma, sending thoughts of love to them wherever they were. She remembered her father teaching from the Talmud that over every blade of grass was an angel whispering, "grow, grow." If that were true, then surely there must be a legion of angels watching over her family.

The plane leveled out at altitude, and the smell of strong coffee made Morgan open her eyes again. Jake brought over a cup of bitter black coffee and they both worked through the stack of research information on Carl Jung, his trip to North Africa, and more images from The Red Book.

Morgan flicked through them and came upon an image of a mandala that reminded her of the one broken during the attack on her office in Oxford. It seemed so long ago now.

She showed it to Jake. "Some scholars think this mandala represented Jung's internal journey in Africa. Perhaps it's some kind of clue to the citadel? The stone should be in the center, representing a spiraling descent into the spirit and soul of each human life."

Jake paged through the notes. "Legend says that

a grandson of Noah founded Nefta after the flood subsided, so it's important to many faiths. When Jung visited, it was peaceful and empty, but with Martin's intel on the extremist group, we're going to need that backup team."

Morgan heard an edge of excitement in Jake's voice at the potential conflict and felt its echo within herself. She relished the thought of some action. After days of running away and being on the back foot, her anger needed an outlet. Everett and Thanatos were the true enemy — but she would let her rage out in Tunisia if that was the only way.

CHAPTER 19

Nefta, Tunisia. May 25

JAKE LAY ON HIS belly on a sand dune over-looking the citadel and the extremist camp below. After meeting the backup team, they had crossed over the border from Algeria and were now almost in position. Jared Rush and his team hid down near the citadel. He was one of ARKANE's senior agents in Africa and a man Jake trusted as a brother. It was good to be out in the field together again.

This citadel, or *ribat*, had been built as part of the military occupation of North Africa by the Muslim empire in the mid-seventh century, used as an outpost for soldiers. These days, a new brand of extremists occupied them once more, intent on spreading their beliefs across the world. Fires burned around the entrance as guards warmed themselves in the chill of the desert night, assault weapons by their sides. But they didn't seem especially vigilant, presuming themselves safe while the focus was on bigger prey in the more dangerous playing fields of Libya and Sudan.

Jake used his night-vision goggles to locate the side entrance of the citadel they had identified from surveillance footage. Jared's team moved into place near the front, ready to draw attention. Jake checked his watch and looked around to make sure the others were ready. Morgan was alert, the black body armor hugging her slight curves, her gaze fixed on the scene below. He could sense her readiness, but despite knowing of her skill in combat, Jake still worried about her safety. That disturbed him because, if he was honest with himself, it was more than a purely operational concern.

He whispered into his headset. "Ninety seconds to go. Be ready to move on my signal."

There were five in their team. Jake and Morgan, and three commandos: Hanson, Margolis, and Tien, part of a special forces group ARKANE called on for some missions. They all wore camouflaged body armor with night-vision goggles, and carried multi-purpose belts with grenades, guns, and tools they might need inside the citadel.

Jared's team fired from the dunes. The guards took cover and then headed toward the attackers, drawn away from the tower entrance.

Jake signaled the advance. He and Morgan ran low and fast toward the citadel, guns at the ready, flanked by the three commandos. They ran through the outer gate, but the guards inside spotted them, raking the scene with a hail of bullets.

The commandos threw grenades and drew their fire, as Jake and Morgan ran for the central tower of the citadel.

A man by the main doorway leapt out at them with a curved blade. Morgan ducked as the weapon swung at her head. Jake slammed into the man with a rugby tackle, smashing his head against the side of a wall.

The attacker lay still as Morgan and Jake fell panting inside the tower entranceway, the sound of gunfire continuing outside.

Moments later, two of the commandos, Hanson and Margolis, collapsed by their side.

"Tien is injured," Hanson reported, "but one of Jared's team picked him up. They should be able to hold the guards off outside for a while, but we need to get in and out as fast as possible in case the militants call for backup."

Jake nodded. "Let's get moving."

Morgan pulled out her phone and flicked to the image of the mandala from The Red Book. "The most precious object is always at the heart, so we should head for the center of the tower."

"Which way?" Jake asked.

The walls were the color of bleached sand, made of enormous blocks hewn from desert stone. Corridors stretched in both directions, curling away from the entrance and in toward the middle of the citadel.

Morgan noticed a mark on the wall and walked closer, running her fingers over the rough-hewn rock that circled the doorway. "Look, a tiny kingfisher, Jung's spirit guide. It must be this way."

She held the phone out to Jake with another image from The Red Book. An old man with turquoise wings the color of a kingfisher standing over a citadel with palm trees on either side, the tangled knot of a snake by his side.

Jake frowned at the snake. "Should we be worried about that?"

Morgan shook her head. "I don't think so. Jung used the serpent motif in many of his images. It represents wisdom and, of course, temptation, as well as the ancient creation story. I'm sure it's allegorical. Let's go."

The corridor wound in to the heart of the citadel,

a tight stone passageway that grew ever narrower, pressing in so they soon had to walk single file. It was a maze of stone, spiraling in on itself, and at each fork, they checked for more symbols, following the tiny kingfisher onward, trusting in Jung's guardian bird.

The corridor opened up into a circular room, with three archways leading away from the central space. Intricate carvings and Arabic script decorated each arch, totally different from what they had seen so far.

They examined the doorways, and Jake shook his head. "There's no kingfisher, only symbols that look like water, air, and fire. Which way should we go now?"

Morgan examined the mandala from The Red Book once more. "The next image seems to be a phoenix, Jung's original family crest, so it must be fire, because the phoenix rose from the flames. But this is only the first symbol. There will be another choice before we reach the center of the citadel."

They walked through the archway marked with fire. Hanson first, followed by Morgan and Jake, with Margolis at the rear.

Their torchlight flickered on the walls as they walked deeper into the heart of the stone castle, the path sloping gently but inexorably down.

A fat-tailed scorpion lurked against one wall, its segmented tail raised in defense, topped by a venomous stinger. Morgan walked carefully around it, acutely aware that its Latin name, *Androctonus*, meant man-killer.

Hanson's voice came from up ahead. "I've found the next split. There are another three archways to choose from."

They filed into the tiny antechamber and checked the doorways. The symbols were more intricately carved this time: creatures crawling in repeated patterns.

Morgan examined them. "A scarab beetle, a snake, and a crocodile."

Margolis cursed. "Oh great, it's just like *The Mummy*. I hate those scarab beetles. We are *not* going that way."

Jake silenced him with a look.

Morgan checked the images from The Red Book once more. "Jung used all these creatures in his drawings. He was fascinated with Egyptian mythology, hence the scarab, and also drew snakes and multi-legged crocodiles in many of his paintings. There's no clear direction here." She ran her fingers along the carvings. "I think we should try the snake. He used that image so much."

Margolis stepped forward. "I'm in. Anything to

avoid that scarab door." He walked through the archway.

Nothing happened.

He took another step, then another one and turned back. "Looks like we're good to—"

The ground disappeared beneath him. Margolis plunged through the hole, his screams echoing through the chamber as he fell.

Jake and Hanson threw themselves down to the floor, reaching for his hand, but there was no way to grab him in time.

His cries grew quieter and eventually faded to nothing. It seemed as if they went on for a long time.

Morgan stood stunned in the antechamber, unwilling to believe Margolis was really gone. Dying in battle was one thing, but falling to your death in an ancient labyrinth was beyond belief — and she had chosen that path. Morgan felt desperately responsible.

She stood frozen, looking down at the hole in horror.

Jake shook her. "Come on, Morgan, we have to get moving or we'll all be in danger. Jared can get a team back in here later with more equipment. They might still find Margolis. Think of Faye. Concentrate: what are we missing?"

Jake was right. Her feelings were a pale shadow of what she would feel if Faye and Gemma went to their deaths because of her failure.

Morgan flicked through the images again and realized that the snake's long, spiral body was an actual pit, not just an allegory. Margolis had fallen into its open maw. After years of seeing Jung's images as purely symbolic, Morgan now struggled to make them fit their physical surroundings. They were representations of this place, embellished with Jung's eclectic mythology.

"The crocodile, it must be. Look at this picture, the crocodile chases the round object. It could be an egg… or a stone."

Jake picked up a rock and threw it into the doorway of crocodiles.

He threw another one, further this time.

Nothing moved.

Hanson slowly stepped through. He inched forward a little way, hugging the wall, tapping the floor in front of him with his foot outstretched in caution.

He shouted back, "I've found the kingfisher again. It must be this way."

They rushed on, and finally found themselves at the entrance of a square room with a stone plinth in the center, carved with snakes. The serpents wound around it, open mouths gaping with fangs bared.

Morgan walked to the pillar and examined the detail. Each snake's head was finely decorated, a perfect replica of a desert killer almost dripping with venom. Their mouths were portals into the depths of the pillar, and she could see something within.

It looked like a box.

She reached out to put her hand into one of the gaping mouths.

Jake grabbed her wrist. "What if it's another trap?"

Morgan angrily pulled her hand from his grasp. "I have to get the stone. This is the room from Jung's painting. Look at the carvings on the checkered floor. The faded turquoise walls. This is where Jung saw fire coming from the stone. It has to be here."

Hanson made a frantic motion with his hand for them to be quiet. Morgan and Jake stood in silence and then heard the noise.

A hissing, slithering sound from behind the walls.

"We have to hurry," Morgan said. "I'm getting that box."

She thrust her hand inside one of the snake's jaws, her heart hammering in fear and expectation that something would bite at any moment. She grabbed the box and pulled her arm back, a sigh of relief on her lips as she extracted it from the pillar.

There was a clunking sound as ancient gears clicked into place.

Jake and Hanson pulled their guns and looked around.

They waited, but nothing happened.

Morgan refocused on the box. It was plain wood, nothing special, just something you might pick up in the souk. She opened it, but her heart sank immediately.

There was no stone inside.

She pulled out a piece of thick sketchpad paper and unfolded it. A crude rendering of the fiery stone image captured in greater detail within The Red Book. Jung must have drawn it here and repainted it later.

It showed a small square room with checkered floor and carved walls, an almost exact replica of where they stood. A man prostrated himself, arms outstretched, before a tiny stone from which emanated a towering pillar of fire.

Morgan read the words written on the page. "*Es ist nicht hier. Es ist mit dem Vater.* Jung's writing in German. It means 'It's not here. It's with the father.' What the hell does that mean?"

"No time for that now. We have to get out of here!" Jake shouted.

Morgan looked up in horror to see desert vipers

slithering from the walls and wriggling from the mouths of the carved pillar.

A scuttling and rattling echoed from behind the rock.

A wave of fat-tailed scorpions poured out of the walls, stingers dripping in venom as they advanced on the team.

CHAPTER 20

THE NIGHTMARE MADE MORGAN'S skin crawl. Snakes she could just about deal with, but scorpions were alien creatures, their armored bodies skittering across the floor in agitation.

She stuffed the box and paper into her jacket, while Jake and Hanson kicked at the creatures and cleared a path to the doorway.

The three of them ran out, back up the winding corridor and sprinting up the steps to the top of the tower that rose above the citadel.

Jake fired a flare high into the air and, from the desert out west, they heard a helicopter coming for them.

Jared's team laid down covering fire, protecting their escape. As the helicopter took off, the team withdrew, overwhelmed by numbers, and headed further into the desert to rendezvous back at the plane.

The helicopter sped away, flying low over the desert, as the sound of gunfire faded into the distance. Morgan stared down at the silver desert, the moonlight slipping across the dunes, pooling in smooth undulations across the expanse below.

She thought of Margolis and her part in his death, for surely it was too late to rescue him now. Guilt twisted her guts. She should have foreseen the traps that awaited them. But through all her studies, Jung's imagery had only ever been read as pure symbolism. If those mandalas represented actual places, what else might that be true of?

Morgan looked over at Jake, his face stony in the moonlight. Margolis was one of his men, and they had not even found another artifact for their efforts. Time was running out to find the final stone.

Once they returned to the plane, Jake went to the back with Jared to debrief the team. There was a heaviness in the atmosphere: grief, but also pragmatism. These men understood that loss was part of the job, but Morgan was determined to make their sacrifice worthwhile.

She sat looking at Jung's handwritten words in a trance of concentration. *It's with the father.* It could be Jung's real father, a significant influence in his life — or his God. But neither made sense with the timeline or with Jung's conflicting spiritual beliefs.

An idea niggled at the back of her mind — but it lay just out of reach.

She calmed her breathing, letting the feelings of guilt subside. As Morgan focused inward, she remembered her father teaching how meditation on specific words could open the mind to an extra dimension. While she never fully embraced his study of Kabbalah, his meditative practices had helped over the years.

She looked at the words on the page, repeating them in her mind, allowing the letters to rise and spin in her imagination until they became a jumble of symbols, meaningless in the void.

The memory clicked into place.

Morgan called Jake over. "I think Jung's stone is in the USA at Clark University in Worcester, Massachusetts. It's the last place where he and the 'father of psychology,' Sigmund Freud, were still on speaking terms."

"What do you mean?" Jake looked tired and beaten down. "The US hasn't come up in any research so far."

Morgan explained. "Jung and Freud went on a trip together with other psychologists in the early 1900s to a conference hosted by G. Stanley Hall. The event introduced psychoanalysis to the Americans, who embraced it wholeheartedly. At that point,

Jung still considered Freud a father figure. He was going to assume the mantle of psychoanalysis in the Freudian tradition — but it was also on that trip that Jung started to discover his own path. He wanted to include the mystic aspect of the human quest in his theories and he believed in so many things that Freud dismissed. Clark University was a turning point, when the father figure was no longer a father. It must be there. Don't you see?"

Jake sat down opposite her and shook his head. "No, I don't see. I'm beginning to doubt this whole Carl Jung connection. We've risked enough, Morgan. I'm not wasting time looking somewhere that might be wrong at this late stage. We should explore other options."

Morgan would not be dissuaded. "I've been to that university hall as part of a centennial celebration in 2009. There's a bust of Freud, pictures of the men together and — most importantly — the twin of this mandala drawn by Jung himself."

She held up the image of the mandala they'd used to navigate the citadel. "That conference was a life-changing event for those psychologists and pivotal to Jung's career. Perhaps he left the stone there for safekeeping away from prying eyes in Europe?"

Jake pulled up their research notes once more and highlighted the dates. "But it confuses the timeline.

It's believed Jung acquired the stone in Tunisia in the 1920s, so he wouldn't have had it with him at Clark in 1909."

Morgan pointed at a later date. "But look, Jung returned to America in 1924. He clearly wanted to hide the stone, but left clues that only his true disciples would understand. I'm sure he would have embraced the role of Keeper. He believed in gnosis, a spiritual knowledge known only to the enlightened few — and he certainly kept secrets."

Jake sighed. "You need to be certain, because we've been wrong before and there are only forty-eight hours until Pentecost dawns in America. This is our last chance."

Morgan closed her eyes for a second and when she opened them again, they were cobalt-blue steel, the violet slash a deeper shade. "Yes, I believe Jung left the stone at Clark. Once we find it, I'll bargain them all for Faye and Gemma. I just want this to be over."

Jake nodded, then directed the crew to fly to America, to Massachusetts.

Clark University, Worcester, Massachusetts, USA. May 26.

They arrived at the airport near Worcester, having slept fitfully on the way over the Atlantic. Morgan drowned her nightmares with several cups of coffee and made a final study of the university plans.

Jake organized the small group. Jared and Hanson would accompany them, their cover as visiting professors with a hastily constructed back story arranged by Martin Klein back at ARKANE. Morgan didn't think they looked much like academics, but no one paid them much attention as they arrived at the imposing main entrance.

The red-brick facade of the main university building rose above them, four stories with large windows looking out over spring-green lawns. The Stars and Stripes flapped in the breeze above an ornate wall clock.

Morgan's body screamed with jet lag. They had covered so many time zones in the last few days. She felt like her soul was still in transit from the desert wadi, and it would be some time before she was a whole person again.

They passed a statue of Sigmund Freud sitting on a stone bench, book in one hand and cane in the other, a commemoration of the 1909 visit. Morgan ran her hand over the cool smoothness of the statue's head, his austere face giving her pause. What if this was the wrong place? They no longer had enough time to make a mistake. She shook her head to clear the lingering doubts, and they progressed into the building.

An enthusiastic student escorted the team straight to the suite of rooms where Jung and other psychologists lectured over one hundred years ago, and left them to their research.

Jared and Hanson remained outside to watch the doors while Morgan and Jake entered the wood-paneled room. Wingback armchairs with maroon leather seats sat around a fireplace that clearly hadn't been used in a while. A square table lay in the center, on top of a circular Turkish rug.

The twin mandala print hung on a far wall, next to the famous picture of the psychologists. They walked closer to examine it.

Morgan flicked to the image of the original on her phone. "There's a difference between the two mandalas."

Jake nodded. "Yes, the wasp in the corner."

Morgan traced the tiny insect with a fingertip. "It's strange because Jung didn't use wasps in his imagery. It seems out of place…"

She shook her head and laughed gently. "Oh,

of course. It must represent Wolfgang Pauli, the Austrian physicist who worked closely with Jung. He won a Nobel Prize for his discovery of the exclusion principle, a key part of quantum physics. There was a strange story about him called the Pauli Effect, where his presence changed things somehow, like equipment breaking as he walked past."

"Do you think this Pauli Effect had something to do with the stone's power?" Jake asked.

Morgan shrugged. "Perhaps. Pauli had a breakdown, and Jung interpreted his dreams. They worked together on ideas about the paranormal and synchronicity, so it's possible he knew about the Pentecost stone and even experienced its power. Maybe he was the one who hid it here."

She frowned. "Pauli was afraid of wasps, and they appeared in his nightmares. Jung interpreted them as a symbol of what he was ultimately scared of — a weapon, the destruction of all that is good in the world."

Jake raised an eyebrow. "You think the Pentecost stones might be this weapon?"

"Maybe. We need to keep looking."

Morgan snapped a picture of the twin mandala and they searched the room carefully, looking for some sign of where the stone might be hidden. Jake lifted the image off the wall, but the frame was empty. They tapped around the wooden panels and checked behind furniture, but found nothing.

Morgan turned around in the center of the room, racking her mind for some other symbol that might show the way.

Then she saw it.

The room was square, a round rug in the center, and a square table in the center of that again.

"This entire room is a mandala, the circle in the square. The center is where truth lies. Help me move this."

They dragged the heavy mahogany table to one side and pulled back the circular rug. A trapdoor lay in the stone floor underneath, engraved with a mandala. Twelve stones spiraled to a copper handle in the center.

Morgan looked up at Jake with a smile. "This has to be it." She bent down to pull the handle.

Gunfire exploded outside the door.

The sound of blows and a scuffle.

"Get down," Jake shouted.

The door burst open and six men rushed in, weapons held high. Morgan and Jake were outnumbered.

CHAPTER 21

THE LEADER OF THE assault was tall with a rangy athleticism and a buzz-cut of silver-grey hair. He wore a black military-style jumpsuit with sleeves rolled up, the pale horse tattoo clear on his forearm.

He pointed at Jake with his gun. "Down on your knees."

As Jake knelt, Morgan hurled herself to the floor, commando rolling toward the leader, drawing his fire.

Shots rang out.

A bullet sliced across Morgan's shoulder, and she spun to the ground, her wound bleeding onto the carpet.

Jake charged and crashed into the leader. He managed to get in a punch before two other men pulled him off. The leader slammed the butt of his gun into Jake's temple, pistol-whipping him to the floor.

As her partner lay on the edge of consciousness, Morgan knew their last stand had been useless — and now she was alone.

The leader bent over Morgan's panting form. "You just made it harder on yourself."

He put his boot onto her shoulder and leaned into the wound. She moaned, almost passing out from the pain, breathing faster as she tried to stay conscious.

He picked up Morgan's backpack and checked inside for the precious cargo. With a smug grin, he slung it over his shoulder. "We'll take the stones from here."

Morgan rolled to her knees, clutching her wounded shoulder. "What about the stones Everett has already?"

"We'll get those too before we return to Europe. The twelve will be together again, but in the hands of true believers, not filth like Everett. He'll pay for crossing Thanatos."

"And my sister and niece?" Morgan dared hope they might be spared.

"I don't have any orders for them. Clearly they're not important."

Morgan breathed a sigh of relief, despite the pain

of her throbbing shoulder. It wasn't over yet. The stones had never been important; it was always about her family.

"Let's find the last stone and get out of here." The leader pointed at Jake's prone body and nodded at one of his men. "Tie him up and keep him for interrogation later. He has valuable information about other ARKANE projects and they'll trade handsomely to get him back."

He knelt and pulled up the trapdoor. It creaked open to reveal a staircase spiraling down into darkness.

The men put on headlamps and dragged Morgan down with them. As she entered the dark portal, her last glance was at Jake, tied and unconscious by the door, blood trickling down his pale face to pool in the carpet beneath him.

The leader forced Morgan ahead. She stumbled in the dark, a cry of pain escaping her lips. "Why do you need me? You can find the last stone yourself."

"We heard about the citadel traps in Tunisia. You're going to make sure we don't have any problems."

"Then what?"

He laughed, pushing her faster down the stairs. "Oh, don't you worry about that. There are plans for you as well as your partner."

They finally reached a small circular chamber at the bottom of the staircase. There was a choice of three doors, just as in Nefta. But this time, they were just plain wood with nothing carved upon them.

Morgan's heart raced. She had made a mistake in Tunisia and it had cost a life. While she certainly wished harm on these men, there was too much at stake to fail. She had to get it right.

"Which door?" the leader said. "Make the right choice, or your friend Jake could have a bullet in the back of his head soon enough."

Morgan pulled out the image of the twin mandala taken in the room upstairs.

As she studied it more closely, she could see more subtle differences from the original. The mandala curled in on itself; the spiral was colored like a map, with line breaks that could indicate choices in the maze. If she followed the openings to the center, perhaps it would lead them to the stone.

The wasp sat in the bottom right of the picture, a beautifully painted tiny nightmare from the mind of Wolfgang Pauli. Morgan's mind raced as she clung to her knowledge of Jung, the doubts swirling about her. But there were no other clues.

She looked up from the mandala. "The middle one."

"If you're lying to us—"

"I just want to find the stone and save my family," Morgan snapped. "Let's get this over with."

The leader raised his hands in mock surrender and nodded to one of his men. "You heard her. Open it."

The door swung open easily to reveal a twisting tunnel with stone walls and a low ceiling. The group moved swiftly on. It seemed to go on a long way. Morgan wondered what was above ground — and why Pauli's nightmare pointed them in this direction.

The passage ended in a final door, carved with twelve stones and wasps weaving around them in a complicated pattern. Stylized flames reached up as if to burn it all away.

The sound of a buzzing hum came from behind the door.

Once again, the images were not pure symbolism. Pauli's weapon was protected by his nightmare.

The leader listened at the door and then shook his head. "A few wasps won't stop us getting the last stone." He nodded at his men. "Go in and get it."

The rest of the team pulled open the door and entered quickly in formation, guns held high as they rushed into the buzzing room.

Morgan caught a quick glimpse inside before the heavy door swung shut. There was a plinth in the middle, lit from a skylight above. Dark shapes hung from the ceiling, surrounded by flying insects, and the floor writhed with more of them.

It was quiet for a few seconds… then the buzzing grew louder.

The sound of gunfire erupted and shouting, screaming — then silence.

The buzzing calmed once more to a gentle hum.

The leader grabbed Morgan and held his gun to her head. "What the hell is in there?"

Morgan's shoulder throbbed with the bullet wound, but despite her pain, a strange sense of calm descended as she contemplated what waited beyond the door. "One of Jung's disciples was a genetic engineer — perhaps they made a hybrid wasp to protect his secret. There are killer wasps in Africa, larger and more vicious. Guns would have little effect on such tiny creatures."

The leader pushed her toward the door, gun still pointed at her head. "I need that stone. You're going in next."

Morgan took a deep breath and considered her knowledge of Jung and Pauli. There must be a way. All these devices allowed the dedicated disciple through unharmed. It was only a trap for those who didn't have the right knowledge, the true gnosis.

The corridor featured in Pauli's nightmares and so did the wasps. She must be missing something.

Morgan looked at the door, focusing on the circle around the wasps in the carving. Perhaps it represented a way to contain the wasps or surround the seeker with protection. The mandala seemed to indicate the door itself was a key of some kind.

She felt around the door frame. On the right-hand side was a slight opening: she reached inside and found a key.

The leader looked puzzled. "The door wasn't locked. Why the key?"

Morgan put her hand on the door handle, ready to go in and face Pauli's nightmare. "Whoever built this must have designed a solution. Perhaps this activates it somehow."

He gave a dark smile. "Whatever you say. Get the stone and I'll wait here. If you don't come out, then I guess it's all over, anyway."

Morgan swallowed. She didn't like wasps, but then, who did? It was a rational human fear. They weren't the subject of her nightmares, but the screams of the dying men who entered before her still echoed in her mind.

A trickle of sweat ran down her back and she clenched her fists in determination. If she died, Faye and Gemma didn't stand a chance.

Morgan took a deep breath, gently pushed open the door, and slid into the room.

The buzzing intensified immediately.

She stood with her back to the door and looked around. Wasps' nests draped from the ceiling and dripped down the walls, hanging almost to the floor. Morgan glimpsed green through the distant skylight, realizing this chamber must be under the Botanical Gardens so the wasps could feed, even as they protected their secret.

The air was thick with flying insects, although many lay dead on the floor next to the bodies of the soldiers. They had stung the men to death, and the corpses were already bloated from the venom.

Wasps crawled over the bodies, crowding on any exposed flesh. One man's face was frozen in a drawn-out scream as a wasp emerged from his swollen mouth. Morgan shuddered. The insects kept their distance for now, and she wondered what made them attack.

There was a stone plinth in the middle of the room, similar to the one in Nefta, but this time, a box lay on top. The Pentecost stone must be in there, but how could she get close enough?

Morgan clutched the key in her hand and dragged her gaze away from the seething mass of writhing gold-and-black insects. If the key didn't open the door, it must fit into a different place.

She looked around for any clue.

Several meters away, on the wall to her right, there were three ornamental mandalas, each with a keyhole in the center.

The ultimate test of the seeker.

If she moved toward the wall, the wasps would surely attack. There would only be a second to place the key in the correct slot before they reached her. She had to choose the right one, or she would die like these men, stung to death, her corpse bloated with venom.

Morgan breathed quietly as the wasps buzzed in swarms just a meter away. A semicircle of light surrounded her from a grille above. It must protect her in some way — but she had to step outside the light to reach the keyholes.

Each mandala was a highly decorated carving with an image at its center, the keyholes part of each intricate design.

On the right, a rainbow of color illuminated the Sephiroth, the tree of life, a Kabbalistic image Jung used in The Red Book. The center mandala was a dark vortex of swirling shades in grey and black with slashes of vermilion. A destructive and almost cruel image, with the keyhole a dark void at its heart. On the left, a many-legged crocodile spun around the keyhole, its limbs dropping off into a pool of blood as a man chopped at them with a sword.

Morgan bit her lip. All were valid aspects of Jung's imagery.

Doubts and fears flooded her mind, images of Faye and Gemma crying, Jake's bloodied face, the bodies they left in their wake — and, as always, Elian's bullet-riddled corpse. She was no stranger to death and she could face her own now.

Morgan made her decision.

She ran forward with the key outstretched in one hand.

As she stepped outside the circle of light, the buzzing grew loud and angry. The wasps took flight.

Morgan reached the wall and plunged the key into the dark vortex of the center mandala. It represented the shadow self, the dark side of the psyche, that must be embraced in order to become whole.

It had to be the correct one.

Morgan felt the brush of tiny furred bodies against her skin and winced at the first sting. A flash of doubt entered her mind as the key plunged inside.

There was a sharp crack as the cavern flooded with light. A high-pitched noise rang out, and she covered her ears.

The wasps dropped out of the air, stunned or dead. Morgan didn't wait to find out if they might recover. She dashed to the plinth, stepping over the bloated corpses and fallen wasps. She opened the box, took out the final Pentecost stone, and ran for the door.

As she flung it open, the leader grabbed her and sprayed a cloud of suffocating fumes into her face.

Morgan coughed and fell to the floor as he took the stone.

Her vision narrowed, and as she sank into inky unconsciousness, the last thing she saw was the pale horse tattoo, a witness to her failure.

CHAPTER 22

IT TOOK A FEW minutes for Jake to come round. His face ached from the blows, his head spun — but he was no stranger to a beating and recovered quickly.

His hands were zip-tied behind him, but his legs were still free. The Thanatos guard crouched down, ready to secure them, his back turned from the captive he thought unconscious.

Jake spun and jack-knifed his body.

He kneed the man in the side of the head, knocking him to the carpet. Jake rolled, using his momentum to kneel astride the guard, pinning his arms by his side.

As the man struggled beneath him, Jake head-butted him. It left him reeling once more, but at least the guard was out cold.

It was over in seconds.

Jake rolled off his prone attacker and lay on the floor, panting from the effort. He listened for any sound outside the door. Footsteps paced up and down. But it sounded like there was only one man.

Jared and Hanson must be down. Jake hoped they were merely injured. The thought of more loss after Nefta was hard to bear.

The trapdoor lay open before him.

Morgan was down there with the other men from Thanatos. His heart beat faster as he thought of her in their brutal hands, but they would keep her alive until they had the stone — and he would need backup to tackle them.

Jake used a knife on the guard's belt to slice open his zip ties, then looked around the room for anything else he could use as a weapon. The dusty shelves contained only old books, but the fireplace had iron tools next to it. A shovel and brush for removing ash — and a poker, its tip hardened by fire.

He picked it up and hefted its weight. He'd have to be fast and accurate. Jake gave a dark smile. Bring it on.

He listened at the door, visualizing the pacing steps. When the guard turned on his patrol, Jake burst through the door and charged.

The guard brought his weapon up.

Jake swung the poker and batted the gun away.

A rattle of bullets peppered the wooden hallway walls — but the guard lost his grip and it fell silent quickly.

Jake tackled him to the floor and used the end of the poker to smash the guard's skull. Once, twice.

The guard went limp, finally unconscious. Jake twisted the guard over and secured him with more zip-ties.

"Jake." The faint voice came from a darkened corner. Jared sat propped up against the wall, one hand over a bleeding wound on his shoulder. Hanson lay prone beside him.

Jake rushed over and checked Hanson's pulse. "He's still alive, but we need medical help."

Jared nodded toward his pack. "I'm pretty sure the authorities have reported gunfire already, but we need a clean-up team. My phone's in there."

Jake rifled through the pack and pulled out the phone. He called Marietti and reported the situation.

"I'll liaise with the authorities," Marietti said, then his tone darkened. "I know you're both injured, Jake, but you need to get those stones. You cannot allow them to be activated at Pentecost."

Jake leaned back against the wall. He had known all along that the mission would have to take precedence over Morgan's family at some point. He just wasn't ready for it yet.

He sighed. "What about Morgan?"

"Dr Sierra has been a valuable asset to the team, but we cannot exchange the stones for her family."

Marietti hung up. Jake grabbed a first-aid kit and did what he could for Hanson, then helped Jared with his injured shoulder. He worked in silence while Jake considered his next inevitable step.

His allegiance was always to ARKANE, but this mission had become personal. Morgan touched something within him, a side that had been dormant for so long. He rarely worked with a partner, and yet she had become one in just a few days. Her intellectual curiosity, her independence and ability to look after herself drew him in — and of course, he found her damn attractive.

Jake finished patching up Jared's shoulder and helped him to his feet. "You okay to go down that trapdoor and finish this?"

Jared nodded. "As ever, my friend."

They grabbed their guns and hurried back into the room. Just then the leader of the Thanatos team emerged from the trapdoor, a pack on his back — and Morgan slumped unconscious in his arms.

Jake and Jared flanked him, guns pointed at his head.

"Put her down," Jake said, the threat clear in his tone. "And she better be unharmed."

The Thanatos leader sighed, resignation in his eyes. He was outnumbered and outgunned, and he knew it. He walked up the last few steps and laid Morgan on the couch. "She's fine. She won't be out long."

He knelt down and put his hands behind his back. Jared tied the man up and dragged him outside the room to join the other guard.

Jake bent to Morgan and checked her pulse. It was strong, and she breathed easily. She would wake soon and he would have to tell her he was leaving with the stones.

Maybe he should just go now and avoid the pain of betrayal, but he needed to know she was okay — and part of him wanted to see her open her cobalt eyes one last time.

Jake stroked her cheek softly. "I'm sorry. I have to do this. There's too much at stake."

He laid his gun on the side table, grabbed the man's pack, and checked the stones. They were all there, including the final piece. Jake couldn't let them join with the ones that Everett held. The risk was too great. He needed to get these back to the vault at ARKANE headquarters in London.

Morgan stirred and moaned a little. Jake returned to her side, bracing himself for what must come.

Morgan came to in a groggy state, her mouth dry, her head throbbing. She opened her eyes to see Jake looking down at her, his face bloody and bruised. He smiled, evidently happy to see her, but there was a distance in his eyes too.

Something had changed.

He helped her sit up. "You're safe. Take it easy now."

Morgan's first thought was of Faye and Gemma. "How long was I out? What time is it? Has Everett phoned with the final destination? When do we leave?"

Jake stood, the backpack of stones in his hand. "It's thirteen hours until Pentecost dawns." He sighed. "But I'm sorry, Morgan. I can't let you take the stones to Everett. The myths are true. They have genuine power. We can't have them loose in the world, especially with the comet approaching its zenith. They'll be safe in the ARKANE vault, safe from Everett — and Thanatos."

It took a second for his words to sink in.

"No!" Morgan sprang off the sofa, rage crushing her physical pain. She was a lioness defending her pride, her family. She would not give up now when she was so close to saving them.

She reached toward Jake, but her legs were still weak. She staggered, and he took a step back, biting his lip, his expression contorted with barely restrained remorse. They had become close. Perhaps too close. Jake had already gone further than he needed to help her, and Morgan felt a glimmer of hope that she could persuade him to stay.

"Please, Jake. Everett is a killer. You saw the videos of the bodies in the fire. My sister and niece will be next if I don't give him what he wants. Please help me."

She reached out to take his hand.

Jake stepped back once more. "The US authorities will rescue Faye and Gemma. It's a simple kidnapping now we've retrieved the stones. They'll be okay, I'm sure."

A wave of nausea swept over Morgan. "There's no time. Pentecost is only hours away."

Jake turned to leave, the backpack in his hand. "I'm sorry, but I have to do this. Come with me and we'll explain everything to the police."

His betrayal cut deep, and Morgan clenched her fists as anger rose within. She should never have trusted him.

As he took a step away, she kicked hard into the back of his knee.

Jake stumbled forward.

Morgan grabbed the lamp from the side table and swung it at his head. "You bastard, you never meant to help me, did you? You used me, just like Ben said you would."

Jake blocked the blow as he fell and twisted on the ground, kicking her legs out from under her so they were both on the floor.

She sprang up again, ready for his attack, ignoring the stabbing pain in her arm and the blinding headache that threatened to overwhelm her.

Jake held out a hand. "This is ridiculous. I will not fight you. I'd help you if I could, but it has to be this way."

Morgan swung at him with her good arm and launched a kick to his head. He blocked it with one muscular arm and Morgan staggered back, bracing herself for another assault.

She would not let him leave with those stones.

As he backed toward the wall, Jake could see the fury in Morgan's eyes as blood soaked the T-shirt at her shoulder. She was like an Amazon warrior in her rage and he admired her loyalty to her family, her ability to fight even when wounded. Hell, he wanted her. This stunning, fiery woman, who attracted him even as she threatened violence.

Morgan swung the lamp again as she stepped closer. The arc was perfect and this time, it connected. Jake's eyebrow split, the pain from his previous wounds intensifying.

Morgan didn't stop. She came at him with a flurry of blows.

Jake had to fight back. He defended himself and blocked Morgan's moves, grateful that her shoulder injury and the aftermath of the drugs weakened her. He wasn't sure he could win a fight against her at full strength.

But time was of the essence. He had to get the stones back to ARKANE.

He punched her wounded arm.

She twisted in agony and sank back down onto the couch, holding her shoulder, her teeth clenched.

Jake couldn't help himself. He went to her and held her close as she gasped in pain. "I'm sorry. Forgive me. I didn't want to hurt you, Morgan, but you've got to stop."

She pulled slightly away from him — then head-butted Jake full on the bridge of his nose.

He reeled back and wiped the dripping blood from his chin.

Morgan jumped up and grabbed the gun from the side table. She pointed it at his head. "I'm taking the stones and saving my family. I will go through you, ARKANE, Everett, Thanatos, whoever I need to, in order to get them back."

Jake dived at her.

He pushed her arm up and the shot went wide into the wall.

He rugby-tackled Morgan and flipped her over roughly, pinning her face down on the carpet. She struggled, but his knee was on her back, her good arm twisted behind in his vice-like grip.

This time, he wasn't letting her up.

Jake grabbed a zip tie and attached one of her wrists to the leg of the couch. "The authorities will be here to help you soon. Everett texted the coordinates. Somewhere near Tucson, Arizona. I know you'll get Faye and Gemma back, but I can't let you take the stones."

Morgan stayed silent, but the betrayal in her eyes said it all. She was bruised, injured, and tied once more, but still strong.

Jake stood for a moment, looking down at her. Perhaps for the last time. She would never forgive his actions today, but he had to leave her behind.

CHAPTER 23

Biosphere 2, Oracle, Arizona, USA. May 27, Pentecost Sunday.

AS DAWN ROSE AND the sun glimmered over the horizon, Joseph Everett walked up through the Biosphere to check on the final preparations for Pentecost. The comet would reach its zenith at eight p.m., when he would perform the sacrifice and call down power from heaven.

He was sure Morgan Sierra would come with the stones. Her sister and niece were the perfect bait.

The Biosphere lay in the little town of Oracle, Arizona, between Tucson and Phoenix, bleached by the high Sonoran desert and overshadowed by the Santa Catalina Mountains. The various sections of the Biosphere mimicked the Earth's existing ecology, housing a self-sustaining ecosystem and a research facility investigating the possibility of living on other planets. The weather inside could be manipulated, and the effects monitored on five separate bio-systems within.

Joseph had purchased the place when it ran into funding difficulties a few years ago. It satisfied the ecological side of his investment portfolio, which was useful in the current political and business environment — but he also enjoyed it for his own private reasons.

He walked up the main path alongside the ocean with its coral reef and passed by the savannah, mangrove swamp, and fog desert. The Biosphere was peaceful, especially at night when Joseph stared up at the stars through the ziggurat of triangular glass and steel panels. He occasionally brought young researchers here to join him when the nights were darkest. Airlocks meant the place was soundproof, and the researchers were paid well to keep quiet about abuses in the dust of the savannah.

As dawn turned to day, the wide expanse of Arizona sky stretched above. The quality of light was stunning inside the complex and, as he walked through the rainforest, Joseph smiled.

He particularly loved being in here during Arizona's more extreme weather conditions. In summer, heat pounded the land — and when the storms came, it was glorious. Web lightning slashed the sky, thunder crashed and rolled down the Sonoran hills, torrential rain carried red dust in streams along the roads.

A reminder of the power of nature to destroy and renew — a fitting place to welcome Pentecost.

With her shoulder patched and out of a sling, dosed up on painkillers, Morgan drove toward the Biosphere.

Her hands lay tight on the wheel of the rental car, her knuckles white as she clenched it, imagining Jake's neck beneath. She had almost let him through her barriers and his betrayal cut deep, but she had to put it aside and concentrate on rescuing Faye and Gemma.

Morgan had escaped Clark University before the authorities arrived, knowing they would only slow her down. Once away from the campus, she called Ben and told him what happened.

He was calm and reassuring in the face of her rage. After all, he had said not to trust ARKANE from the beginning. Ben had contacts all over the Christian world and sent her to a Teresian Carmelite convent in a nearby town. He called in a few favors and arranged a flight to Arizona and funds for the journey.

She had rented a car at the airport and could still make it to the Biosphere by the early evening of Pentecost just before the zenith of the comet. With a gun in the holster at her back and the cool of a knife strapped against her calf under her jeans, Morgan dared hope she might be able to rescue her family alone.

She stopped on the drive and collected rocks from the roadside, roughly the size of the Pentecost stones. It wouldn't fool Everett for long, but it might at least buy her some time.

The desert was scrubland near the city, but as Morgan drove out from Tucson toward Catalina and then Oracle, hills overshadowed the road. Clouds scudded across the sky, the wind whipping them into peaks of fluffy white. A red-tailed hawk hovered overhead, wings barely moving as it rode the currents.

Morgan was at home in this terrain. It reminded her of the desert around the cities of Israel — where she had often driven into danger during her time with the military. Although some of her memories were harrowing, Morgan felt alive out here once again, a far cry from the suffocating rules and safety of academia back in Oxford. This mission had freed her in so many ways, but she would think about her career later. Right now, it was all about her sister and niece.

Faye didn't have Morgan's military experience, but she certainly had a strong faith. Her sister was like the reeds that grew by the River Cherwell in Oxford, anchored deep in faith, bending but never breaking in the storms and hail.

"Hold on, Faye," Morgan whispered, as the white domes of the Biosphere gleamed in the distance, and beyond them, thick purple clouds swollen with rain.

A storm was coming.

Faye stood by the sink in the Biosphere living area, peeling carrots for dinner.

While in captivity, she kept up a routine of domestic chores to behave normally for Gemma, who played beside her on the tiles, singing nonsense songs to herself. They had been inside the human habitat of the Biosphere for several days, and no one had visited since the airlock closed upon them. It was comfortable enough and there were provisions, even books and films to keep them occupied.

It could certainly be a lot worse.

Faye hadn't seen Joseph Everett since the trip out to the kiln. After that terrifying day, she clung to Gemma, desperate to get her to safety, but there had been no chance to escape, and Faye couldn't fight while her daughter was at risk.

When she closed her eyes at night, she saw the face of the burning man in the kiln, his skin crackling, his screams haunting her. The flames of memory licked her skin, and she prayed Morgan was on her way. Her sister was resilient, and with her military experience, Faye was sure Morgan would come for them. She could only hope it would be in time.

The door slammed open.

Faye snatched Gemma into her arms and held her close.

Two guards stood at the door, guns at their belts. One beckoned. "It's time to go. Hurry now. He's waiting for you."

Gemma whimpered, and Faye cuddled her daughter closer as she walked between the guards into the main dome of the Biosphere, trying not to imagine what awaited them.

They stumbled through the rainforest and up to a platform at the highest point. It overlooked the mesa and the ocean with a view out through the glass onto the desert, where the sun dipped toward the horizon.

A rectangle of stacked wood dominated the platform, with a bed of thinner logs on top, wide enough for a person to lie on. Ropes hung down on either side.

It was a funeral pyre.

Faye gasped and clutched Gemma even closer.

Joseph Everett stood next to the pyre with another man in a wheelchair by his side. He was clearly Joseph's twin, a pale, skeletal version of their captor, staring vacantly into the distance, untethered to this world.

Joseph beckoned to Faye. "Come. Look closer. I made the pyre with wood from all kinds of holy places, as befitting a woman of faith. A perfect offering to God on this day of healing and resurrection — through inevitable destruction."

"What do you want from me?" Faye whispered. "What are you going to do with my daughter?"

He gestured at the pyre. "Your sacrifice to the flames will amplify the stones, as I call down the power of Pentecost at the zenith of the comet." Joseph pointed at the wheelchair-bound man. "This is my brother, Michael. The stones will heal him tonight."

"No!" Faye cried and held her daughter even closer. She turned to run, but the guards grabbed her and held her fast. "Just let Gemma go. Please. I'm begging you. She's only a baby."

Joseph shrugged. "I might let her go if your sister shows up and you both accept your fate. A sacrifice of twins would be the most fitting, after all. But now we must prepare."

He motioned to the guards.

One tore Gemma from Faye's arms. The little girl screamed and reached out to her mother. Faye tried desperately to get to her. The guard held a cloth over the little girl's mouth, and Gemma sank into unconsciousness.

Faye stopped struggling, a sudden calm washing over her. At least Gemma would not see whatever happened next.

She met Joseph's gaze. "You're wrong about the stones. There's no human sacrifice in the Christian tradition — and no power of healing except from God Himself."

Joseph pulled open his shirt, revealing the pendant hanging around his neck. "The stones are made of a unique radioactive rock that resonates with the Resurgam comet. Whether the death and resurrection of Jesus originally empowered them is unknown, but the healing powers of the Apostles certainly came from these stones. Today, for only the second time in history, they will be together once more."

A radio crackled, and the voice of another guard came over the line. "She's here."

Joseph smiled. "Excellent. Morgan is just in time — and she's alone."

Faye collapsed to the ground, head in her hands,

as she desperately prayed for God to intervene. If Morgan was alone, then it was over.

They would all die tonight.

The guards hoisted her up onto the pyre and tied her wrists to the heavy logs. Faye screamed in terror, the thought of flames consuming her flesh too much to bear.

CHAPTER 24

As Morgan entered the Biosphere — the bag of rocks clutched in one hand, a gun in the other — she heard her sister scream.

"Faye!" she shouted, just as two guards stepped out from behind the trees.

They took her gun and roughly pushed her up through the Biosphere ecosystem. Morgan scanned the way for escape routes and possible weapons, but there was nothing she could use.

The guards shoved Morgan onto the platform at the top of the rainforest habitat. Faye lay shackled on a funeral pyre and Gemma was curled unconscious on the ground, guarded by more armed men.

Joseph Everett stood next to a man in a wheelchair, presumably his brother, Michael. "I'm so glad you could make it. Let me see the stones."

Morgan clutched the bag tightly. "Let Faye down

first. You can have the stones in exchange for my family, as you promised. Backup is coming."

Joseph laughed at her bluff. "We know ARKANE abandoned you — and my plans have changed."

The guard behind punched Morgan hard in the kidneys. She fell to her knees with the pain, her body exhausted and broken from the beatings and bullets she had suffered over the last few days.

The guard punched her to the ground, and she rolled on her side, holding the bag of stones close to her body.

Joseph leaned down and held a gun to her forehead. "It's time to give them up, Morgan. I can shoot you in the head and burn your niece instead. I don't need you."

Morgan released the bag.

"Excellent. Let's take a look." Joseph emptied the bag out on a table next to the stones he already had — and a Geiger counter to measure the radioactivity of the unique rocks.

He realized the trick within seconds. "Where are they? Did you come all this way just to die?"

In fury, he kicked Morgan repeatedly, landing his boots wherever he could. Morgan heard Faye screaming her name as her world slipped away.

"I'd stop that if I were you."

The deep voice came from the edge of the

rainforest. A wave of relief swept over Morgan, even in the depths of her pain. Jake had come back for her.

Jake held a gun to the head of the guard in front of him and a bag in his hand. "I have the real Pentecost stones. Let them all go and you can have them."

Joseph growled deep in his throat. "I don't bargain for what is rightfully mine."

He grabbed a gun from the table and shot the man Jake held as a shield.

Jake fired in return, a double tap, killing the two guards who raced toward him — but a bullet hit Jake's hand.

He dropped the stones and ducked away into the undergrowth of the rainforest. The remaining guards charged after him.

"Kill him!" Joseph shouted as he climbed down from the platform and swept up the bag. "I will have my sacrifice."

Jake ran through the thick foliage that slapped at his body as he pushed deeper into the rainforest.

It was dense with liana and palms, dripping with water that rained down constantly on the ecosystem, the smell of wet earth a tangy reminder of the jungles of Borneo. Jake had to draw the guards away and lose them in this maze of trunks and vines — then he could double back to the pyre.

He had gone directly against Marietti's orders by coming here, but Jake would not leave Morgan alone again. After he left her in Worcester, he was haunted by visions of his family, hacked to bloody limbs in South Africa by a gang high on methamphetamines. If he had been there, perhaps he could have saved them — or died alongside them.

Some days, Jake wished for that outcome.

When he thought of Morgan heading to almost certain death, risking her life for Faye and Gemma, he had to come after her. Perhaps helping save her family might go some way to assuaging the guilt he felt about his own. He would face the consequences back at ARKANE — if he made it back.

Jake ducked behind a palm tree as the guards crashed through the undergrowth after him. Wind blew outside and rattled the Biosphere glass as rain hammered down. The storm was fast approaching.

Grabbing the end of a liana, Jake wrapped it around his uninjured hand and waited for the guards.

As they ran past on the narrow boardwalk, Jake leapt out and wound the vine around the last man's neck.

A quick flick and Jake pushed him off the board-walk, the man's fingers scrabbling at the constricting vine as he choked.

The other guard turned and shot wildly, bullets pinging against the hardwood trees.

Jake dived for the man's legs and toppled him to the ground. In a wrestler's grip, he flipped the man over and slammed his head hard down onto the boardwalk.

The body went limp.

An agonized scream pierced the sound of the rising storm.

As Faye screamed, Morgan groaned and rolled over onto her side, sharp pain stabbing through her ribs and into her chest. She was wounded, but not out just yet.

Joseph examined the real stones at the table near the pyre, checking each with the Geiger counter. By the look on his face, they were real.

He glanced over at her. "It seems we will have our sacrifice today, after all. The stones will heal Michael and we shall be true brothers once more."

Gunfire echoed from down in the rainforest.

Joseph smiled. "Your partner is gone, Morgan. It's time to summon the power of Pentecost."

He wheeled his brother closer to the pyre, then placed all but the largest of the stones in a mesh bag and draped it around Michael's neck. He wiped some drool tenderly from his brother's mouth. "Not long now. Soon you'll be restored to me."

In that moment, Morgan understood Joseph's actions stemmed from a deep love of his wounded brother. He would do anything to save what remained of his family — and they certainly had that in common.

Joseph lit a taper and held it to the bottom of the pyre. As the flames caught, Faye screamed once more.

A heavy lid of storm clouds dropped over the Biosphere and turned the sky black from the nearby town of Oracle to as far away as Tucson in the Catalina foothills. Lightning flickered in the gloom, metallic blue streaks against the burnt-orange sky lit by the last rays of the smothered sun.

Purple sheets of rain bruised the land, punishing the saguaro cacti as they raised their dusty grey arms to God like desperate believers. Crimson and silver-blue cracks broke the clouds and hurtled to earth, the jagged lightning strikes ever closer to the stepped ziggurat of the Biosphere.

A rumble of thunder rattled the windows of the adobe houses nearby and high above the clouds, in an event not seen for two thousand years, the eye of the comet storm reached the Earth's atmosphere.

Joseph laughed and raised his arms to the sky. "It has begun. The twelve are reunited. I call their power down from heaven."

The wind grew in intensity and rain pounded the Biosphere, engulfing it in fury. The steel-and-glass structure creaked and moaned, struggling to hold together beneath the ferocity of the storm.

Lightning crackled, luminous veins connecting sky to earth as electricity supercharged the air. The first strike hit the north side of the Biosphere ziggurat, lighting the rainforest in brilliant magnesium white, the deep explosion of thunder immediately behind.

The storm was upon them.

Forked lightning split the sky, visible branches breaking into splinters of light while thick bolts smashed into the glass and steel. Wind spun around the building, encasing the Biosphere in its own hellish vortex.

Cracks appeared in the glass and spread quickly, raining shards down on the remaining guards.

Joseph seemed unaware of the destruction, reveling in the storm's power as his men ran for the exits, unwilling to risk their lives any further.

As rain poured in through broken glass, the

wind whipped around them, and Joseph held up his hands to the unseen forces, his voice drowned by the storm.

The stones glowed around Michael's neck as if sculpted from volcanic magma, torn from deep inside the Earth. Joseph held the largest in his outstretched hands toward the splintering roof.

Morgan rolled over and crawled slowly but surely while Joseph was distracted, focused only on the stones and the storm. She climbed onto the pyre behind Faye and pulled the knife from her boot.

She cut the bonds that held her sister to the smoldering pyre, the smoke of wet wood hiding their actions.

They dropped off the edge of the pyre and crawled together to where Gemma lay motionless by the edge of the rainforest, soaked by the rain. Faye lifted her daughter into her arms, rocking her in relief.

Morgan turned to see Joseph and Michael surrounded by brilliant light, the stones alive in balls of flame but somehow not burning their flesh. The brothers together at last in one final attempt at salvation.

Faye headed down the hill, stumbling a little. Morgan reached for her arm and supported her weight. They hurried down the path together as the storm raged about them.

Jake emerged from the rainforest and swept Gemma into his powerful arms so Morgan could help Faye down the stairs. He met Morgan's eyes briefly, and she nodded. No time for words. It was enough that he had come back for her.

They ran together down through the rainforest, past the ocean, and onto the desert mesa. No one stopped them. The guards had deserted Joseph as the end seemed in sight and the Biosphere was clearly failing structurally in the face of the tempest.

As they reached the exit, the creaking of the structure turned to a mechanical scream. The supports began to break and buckle under the dense rain and hail, lightning super-heating the steel.

As they ran from the building, a bolt of pure scarlet scythed apart the clouds above the Biosphere.

Morgan turned to see it strike the platform where Joseph stood next to Michael, his hands on his brother's shoulders. The light flickered around them gently, then whirled into a pillar of flame connecting heaven to earth. Michael rose from his chair and embraced his twin, the brothers frozen in ruby light from above that split into a million drops as rain hammered down.

A moment later, it exploded in brilliant shards and the brothers were lost in the glare.

Morgan blinked and shook her head. Had she really seen a miracle deep in the flames?

As the Biosphere collapsed, crushing everything within, she ran out into the rain to be with her family once more.

Firefighters and police soon arrived at the Biosphere, drawn by the storm and the inferno witnessed across the desert from the town of Oracle. An ambulance crew rushed to meet the survivors as they emerged from the dome, coughing in the smoke.

Jake squeezed Morgan's hand, then disappeared toward the police vehicles. A paramedic worked on Gemma as Morgan held her sobbing sister close. She called David, handing the borrowed phone to Faye when her husband answered with a sob of relief.

Morgan left them to talk and turned to watch as the remains of the Biosphere burnt furiously in the night, the fires still fierce even in the bucketing monsoon. She held her face up to the storm, the wash of cool rain running down her neck, hiding her tears of relief that it was over.

Hours later, Morgan sat in one of the Biosphere's outlying adobe houses, watching Faye and Gemma sleeping on a bed. Faye was curled around her little girl in a protective shield, and Morgan reached out to gently brush a curl from her sister's forehead.

It was time to go home. But first, she needed to find Jake.

Morgan checked her reflection in a mirror by the rough wall. She was bruised and bloody from the beatings, her eyes bloodshot, her skin still sooty with ash. Her arm was in a new sling but her T-shirt was dirty and she smelled of smoke.

Morgan smiled. She didn't look like an academic anymore — and she was glad of it. Despite Jake's betrayal, he had returned and their mission together had helped her rediscover this side of herself.

Morgan walked out into the Arizona dawn as the first rays of sun inched over the horizon. Fires still smoldered in the wreckage of the Biosphere and firefighters sifted through the ash, looking for evidence.

Jake stood at the edge of the debris, bruised muscles in his back visible through his torn, sooty shirt. There was so much Morgan wanted to say. The only question was whether she could speak the words aloud.

She walked over and Jake turned, silhouetted against the russet sky. "How are Faye and Gemma?"

"They're sleeping. They'll be okay." She took a deep breath. "Jake—"

"Morgan—"

They spoke at once. Laughing together, they turned back to look at the shattered ruins, the moment broken.

"They only found one skeleton," Jake said.

Morgan frowned. "How can that be? Nothing could have survived that inferno."

Jake shrugged. "We've seen some strange things tonight, that's for sure."

Morgan stared out into the destruction. "What about the stones?"

"I'll find them, don't worry. It's time you took your family home."

As the last of the fires burned to ash, Jake reached for Morgan's hand. She entwined her fingers with his, united for a moment at the end of the storm.

CHAPTER 25

London, England. Two weeks later

MORGAN STOOD IN TRAFALGAR Square, debating whether she wanted to go through with this.

ARKANE Director Elias Marietti had invited her to London for a mission debriefing. She'd accepted out of a desire for closure — and if she was honest, part of her wanted to see Jake again. Much remained unsaid between them and she hadn't spoken to him since Pentecost. She wondered whether he'd found the stones, or whether the inferno had destroyed them along with the Biosphere.

There was only one way to find out.

She walked to the official entrance of ARKANE, where Marietti's secretary met her and escorted Morgan to the director's office.

Marietti rose to greet her and indicated a chair.

"You've been a great asset, Morgan. Thank you for helping in our mission to retrieve the Pentecost stones."

Morgan remained standing. "You're mistaken. I only wanted to rescue my family. You would have sent them to their deaths."

Marietti gave a thin smile as he sat down. "We all have to make our choices. But you're intrigued by ARKANE, aren't you? You saw evidence of another reality in the flames, and that's just a hint of what we do here. There are always new mysteries to solve."

Morgan crossed her arms. "Why are you telling me this now?"

Marietti leaned back in his chair, meeting her enquiring gaze. "I want you to join us."

A sharp intake of breath came from behind her.

Morgan turned to see Jake in the doorway. He was clean shaven and wore a slate-grey suit, his corkscrew scar standing out against tanned skin. He was a handsome incarnation of the man she'd traveled with, who had been beaten, shot, and stained with ash from the flames of Pentecost. But this man was a stranger, his face stony, and the Jake she had glimpsed in the ruins of the Biosphere lay hidden once more.

Marietti ignored his entrance and continued. "We need a researcher who can help us solve these mysteries, someone with your expertise in biblical history and psychology of religion. We also need someone who can hold her own as a field agent — and you can clearly do that."

Morgan considered the incredible resources of ARKANE, the secrets they protected, the missions she might experience as part of the organization. Marietti certainly knew how to tempt her professional side.

She had only been in academia a short while, but Morgan longed for adventure. This mission had been a glimpse of a possible life — but then she considered what Faye and Gemma had suffered, and how close she had come to the flames of Everett's fire and the bullets of Thanatos.

Marietti held up his hand. "Think about it. Take some time. But first, have a look at this."

He picked up a plain black case of dark wood, inscribed with tongues of fire picked out in gold leaf. Marietti laid it on the table and opened the lid.

"You found the stones?" Morgan exclaimed, amazed they had been pulled intact from the flames. The stones lay benign, just twelve pieces of rock, each with the name of its saint carved above.

She recognized her stone and remembered when her father had given it to her, back when she had no hint of what powers it might contain. "This one is mine — and that is my sister's. You have no right to keep them."

"But you appreciate their potential power now," Marietti said. "It's best they rest together in our vault. No one will come for you or your family while we keep them safe here."

Morgan reached out and traced the outline of her stone with a fingertip. Then she nodded and closed the lid.

Marietti stood. "You deserve to see them laid to rest. Come, we'll go down together."

Marietti led the way and Morgan picked up the case, her fist tight around the handle. She glanced sideways at Jake as they entered the elevator. He seemed so distant. Had he moved on so soon? Was she just part of the mission to him?

They descended into the depths of the ARKANE vaults and Marietti stopped in front of an ancient portal, inlaid with modern steel bars and protected by a high-level security system. Marietti scanned his retina and entered a passcode. Jake followed suit to authenticate the entry. The doors opened.

Marietti waved Morgan inside. "Few outsiders see this, but I thought you'd find it interesting."

A puff of cool air blew over them from the humidity-controlled vault as they walked through the doors. Morgan marveled at the size of the hall in front of her. It stretched into the distance; opaque, sealed rooms on either side concealed untold treasures within.

"This is where we keep the most precious and dangerous artifacts," Marietti said. "Manuscripts of heresy and occult knowledge, the bones of martyred saints — secrets the world would have us keep."

"Or you would keep from the world," Morgan countered as they walked further in.

Marietti stopped in front of a small doorway and led her inside. A shrouded light outlined boxes, paintings, and scrolls, all in numbered niches around the walls. "The stones can rest easy alongside these secrets."

He indicated a section for the case, but Morgan didn't relinquish it.

"After what you've put me through, after leaving my family to die, how can you ask me to give the stones back? There's more to ARKANE than protecting religious secrets for the good of humanity, I know that, but why should the stones stay with you?"

Marietti sighed; his shoulders slumped and age showed in his face. "We couldn't let the power of the stones into the world, and you're a resourceful woman. Clearly, you inspired great loyalty in Jake, and you both made it out with the stones, so no harm done — this time, at least. They are safe here, and if you work with us, they will be close by. Think about it, Morgan. You're a scholar. You seek knowledge… but perhaps adventure as well."

Morgan looked around the vault at the cornucopia of intoxicating possibility. After a moment of deliberation, she bent and gently laid the case down in its allotted place.

They walked out of the vault, and Morgan turned to Marietti. "This ARKANE life has too high a price. I'm going back to my family and Oxford."

She looked pointedly at Jake. He met her eyes with a challenge, saying nothing to stop her.

Morgan turned away and walked down the long corridor, back toward the elevator.

Marietti called after her. "A war is coming, Morgan. A religious battle in which millions may die, and only ARKANE can stop it. Thanatos will regroup and we believe their most deadly assault is ahead of us. We need you."

Morgan paused at his words. Something about them rang true, and she wondered if death would stalk her, regardless of her choice. Would her family be safer if she became an ARKANE agent? Or was she just tempted by the possibilities it offered?

"Ask Ben," Marietti said. "Ask him about your parents and the pale horse of Thanatos. You heard the prophecy, that the stones will be together in the end times. Those times are upon us. Ask Ben and then call me."

Morgan walked on, faster now, away from his haunting voice. Up in the elevator, through the levels of ARKANE, and back out into the light of another London day.

The ARKANE adventures continue in
CRYPT OF BONE.

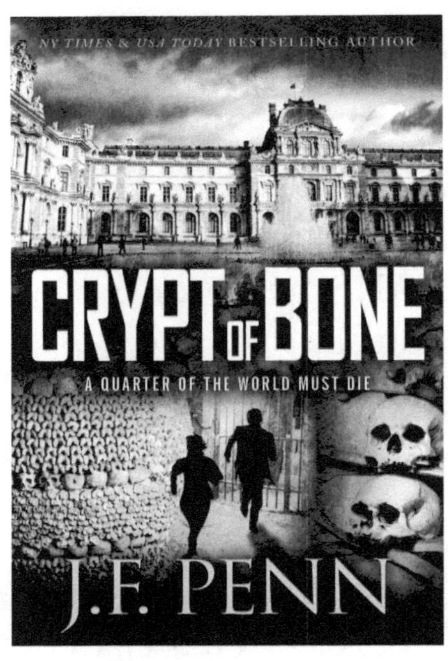

Two billion people are about to die…
and they're the lucky ones.

When a man in a hospital gown jumps to his death from the Western Wall in Israel, the authorities think it's just another victim of Jerusalem Syndrome: a religious psychosis triggered by a visit to the holy city.

But when a second victim ritually disembowels himself, it's the sign of much worse to come. Thanatos — a fanatical group dedicated to the destruction of the world — is on the move again.

The only ones who can stop them are ex-Israeli

military psychologist, Oxford professor, and religious expert Morgan Sierra; and Jake Timber, agent of ARKANE, the British agency tasked with investigating — and sometimes saving the world from — the supernatural.

Last time, Morgan and Jake worked together to stop Thanatos from bringing about a dark version of Pentecost. This time, Thanatos is mixing science with sacrilege — combining the Devil's Bible with mind-control technology to murder a quarter of the human race.

Together, Morgan and Jake will travel from the hallowed halls of Oxford, to the labs of a biotech company with a dark agenda, to a chapel made of human bones. They'll go anywhere, do anything, to stop Thanatos.

But they have to hurry.

Thanatos is on the rise. Apocalypse is at the gates. And the only way to save a quarter of the world is for Morgan to uncover the secrets of her past… at the cost of her own future. Death awaits in a Crypt of Bone.

New York Times and USA Today bestselling author J.F. Penn draws you deeper into darkness with *Crypt of Bone*, the second of the ARKANE adventures.

Available now:
www.books2read.com/cryptofbone

You can also sign up for J.F. Penn's Reader List
and receive another free ARKANE thriller at
www.jfpenn.com/free

ENJOYED STONE OF FIRE?

If you loved the book and have a moment to spare, I would really appreciate a short review on the page where you bought the book. Your help in spreading the word is gratefully appreciated and reviews make a huge difference to helping new readers find the series. Thank you!

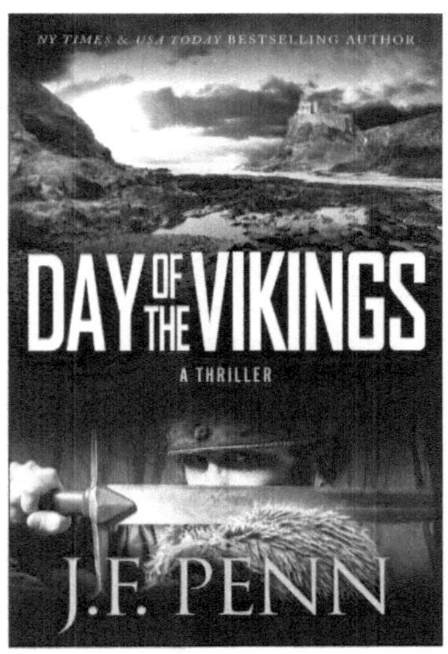

Get a free copy of the bestselling thriller, *Day of the Vikings*, ARKANE book 5, when you sign up to join my Reader's Group. You'll also be notified of new releases, giveaways and receive personal updates from behind the scenes of my thrillers.

WWW.JFPENN.COM/FREE

Day of the Vikings, an ARKANE thriller

A ritual murder on a remote island under the shifting skies of the aurora borealis.

A staff of power that can summon Ragnarok, the Viking apocalypse.

When Neo-Viking terrorists invade the British Museum in London to reclaim the staff of Skara Brae, ARKANE agent Dr. Morgan Sierra is trapped in the building along with hostages under mortal threat.

As the slaughter begins, Morgan works alongside psychic Blake Daniel to discern the past of the staff, dating back to islands invaded by the Vikings generations ago.

Can Morgan and Blake uncover the truth before Ragnarok is unleashed, consuming all in its wake?

Day of the Vikings is a fast-paced, supernatural thriller set in London and the islands of Orkney, Lindisfarne and Iona. Set in the present day, it resonates with the history and myth of the Vikings.

If you love an action-packed thriller,
you can get Day of the Vikings for free now:

WWW.JFPENN.COM/FREE

Day of the Vikings features Dr. Morgan Sierra from the ARKANE thrillers, and Blake Daniel from the London Crime Thrillers, but it is also a stand-alone novella that can be read and enjoyed separately.

AUTHOR'S NOTE

Thank you for joining Morgan and Jake
on the hunt for the Pentecost stones. I hope you
enjoyed the adventure!

The story is based on historical research spun into fiction, as well as my travels to places of religious and cultural significance. Here are some of the influences for *Stone of Fire*, and you can see related images at www.pinterest.co.uk/jfpenn/stone-of-fire

The Pentecost stones and the Apostles after the book of Acts

The biblical book of Acts chapter two describes the day of Pentecost when the Holy Spirit was poured out on the Apostles of Jesus, but there is no biblical tradition of any stones taken from the tomb. Pentecost seems to be the last time the Apostles were together in one place as the twelve subsequently scattered across the known world, so it's certainly possible that they took symbols of brotherhood with them.

I used multiple sources to locate the likely resting places of the stones if they were kept with the bodies of the Apostles. Some are well known, like James and Peter, but others disappeared into myth, like Simon the Zealot.

If you're interested in learning more, check out *The Search for the Twelve Apostles* by William Steuart McBirnie.

Resurgam comet

The Resurgam comet is fictitious, although I based the idea on aspects of comet Elenin, which passed close to the Earth in 2011 during the period of the earthquake and tsunami in Japan.

The related biblical verses are Mark chapter 13, Matthew 27:51–52, 28:2, Revelation 6:12–14.

India

Bodies are burnt at Manikarnika ghat in Varanasi, and Hindus believe they can escape the endless cycle of rebirth if they die there. I watched the burning bodies at night from a boat on a trip in 2006, and as a Westerner, where death is mostly hidden, it was a profound experience.

I return to Varanasi and other locations in India in *Destroyer of Worlds*.

England

Oxford is steeped in myth and history and crops up in many of my books. Morgan's office in Bath Place is a real location, but it's actually a hotel. The Turf Pub is just behind it and well worth visiting for a beer.

Blackfriars is on St Giles, and I attended tutorials there when I studied theology at Mansfield College in the 1990s, but I've taken liberties with the interior and layout. The Pitt Rivers Museum is a treasure trove of inspiration that you can roam online as well as in the flesh. www.prm.ox.ac.uk

Trafalgar Square in London is well known as a tourist destination — but who knows the truth of what lies beneath!

You can listen to a personal account of my time at the University of Oxford at www.booksandtravel. page/oxford

Spain

Santiago de Compostela has a silver reliquary of St James and also the largest swinging censer in the world, the Botafumeiro. The vision of Pope Leo XIII was based on real Church archives.

The ARKANE adventures continue in Spain in *Gates of Hell.*

Iran

There is a church of St Mary in Tabriz, and the Armenian faith is one of the oldest in the world. I took liberties with the location, as there was little definite information, but one or more of the Apostles certainly made it that far east.

Morgan and Jake return to Iran in *Tree of Life.*

Italy

The Pope leads mass in St Peter's regularly. My husband and I attended Epiphany in January 2010, which inspired the scene.

There is a glass case holding the remains of Pope Pius X, and the statue of Alexander features a skeleton with an hourglass.

Venice floods every year and may indeed be underwater one day, hopefully not in our lifetime. There is a spectacular Pentecost mural in the Basilica San Marco, which reshaped the entire plot after our visit there.

Amalfi is the supposed resting place of St Andrew and I've walked through the lemon groves above the town — although personally, I prefer gin to limoncello!

Israel

I am perpetually inspired by Jerusalem, having traveled there several times. The church of the Holy Sepulchre is as chaotic as I describe, and the Ethiopian Coptics have a chapel on the roof. Israel appears in many more ARKANE thrillers, particularly *Gates of Hell* and *End of Days*.

Tunisia

The wadi at Nefta is real, but everything about the citadel is fictional.

USA

The founders of modern psychology did indeed visit Clark University in 1909, and there is a statue of Freud on a bench.

I once visited the Biosphere in Arizona and the glass ziggurat came to mind as somewhere that would explode dramatically, and the storms in Arizona make the strange weather a possibility. You can find more information at www.biosphere2.org

Morgan and Jake return to the USA together and separately in *One Day in New York* and *Valley of Dry Bones*.

Carl Jung, The Red Book, and Wolfgang Pauli

Psychology is one of my abiding fascinations, particularly as it relates to religion and faith. I studied Carl Jung at university and almost trained as a psychologist — but that would have been another life!

The Red Book was revealed to the public in 2009, and I have an oversized copy. It contains a painting by Jung of a pillar of fire spouting from a grey stone in a room as described. But of course, the interpretation is my own.

Jung traveled to North Africa, North America, and Clark University. He counseled physicist Wolfgang Pauli on his dreams, and the wasp was an actual nightmare. The relationship of these men to the Apostles of Jesus is fictional — as far as I know!

MORE BOOKS BY J.F.PENN

ARKANE Action-Adventure Thrillers

Stone of Fire #1
Crypt of Bone #2
Ark of Blood #3
One Day In Budapest #4
Day of the Vikings #5
Gates of Hell #6
One Day in New York #7
Destroyer of Worlds #8
End of Days #9
Valley of Dry Bones #10
Tree of Life #11
Tomb of Relics #12

Brooke and Daniel Psychological/Crime Thrillers

Desecration #1
Delirium #2
Deviance #3

Mapwalker Dark Fantasy Adventures

Map of Shadows #1
Map of Plagues #2
Map of the Impossible #3

Short Stories

A Thousand Fiendish Angels

The Dark Queen

A Midwinter Sacrifice

Blood, Sweat, and Flame

Other Books

Risen Gods — co-written with J. Thorn

American Demon Hunters: Sacrifice —
co-written with J. Thorn, Lindsay Buroker,
and Zach Bohannon

More books coming soon …

You can sign up to be notified of new releases,
giveaways and pre-release specials - plus, get a free
ebook!

www.JFPenn.com/free

If you loved the book and have a moment to spare,
I would really appreciate a short review on the
page where you bought the book.

Your help in spreading the word is gratefully
appreciated and reviews make a huge difference to
helping new readers find the series.

Thank you!

ABOUT J.F.PENN

J.F. Penn is the Award-nominated, New York Times and USA Today bestselling author of the ARKANE action adventure thrillers, Brooke & Daniel Psychological Thrillers, and the Mapwalker fantasy adventure series, as well as other standalone stories.

Her books weave together ancient artifacts, relics of power, international locations and adventure with an edge of the supernatural. Joanna lives in Bath, England and enjoys a nice G&T.

You can follow Joanna's book research and travels on Instagram and Facebook @jfpennauthor and also on her podcast at BooksAndTravel.page or on your favorite podcast app.

* * *

Sign up for your free thriller,
Day of the Vikings, and updates from behind the
scenes, research, and giveaways at:

www.JFPenn.com/free

*   *   *

Connect with Joanna:
www.JFPenn.com
joanna@JFPenn.com
www.Facebook.com/JFPennAuthor
www.Instagram.com/JFPennAuthor
www.BooksAndTravel.page

*   *   *

For writers:

Joanna's site, www.TheCreativePenn.com empowers authors with the knowledge they need to choose their creative future. Books and courses by Joanna Penn, as well as the award-winning *Creative Penn Podcast* provide information and inspiration on how to write, publish and market books, and make a living as a writer.

ACKNOWLEDGMENTS

Thank you to everyone who has encouraged me during the writing of the book, especially to all the enthusiastic readers on my blog, TheCreativePenn.com. Your comments, tweets and emails in the last year of writing have made it a journey I've been privileged to share. Your votes for the book cover and comments on the back blurb in particular helped me no end and I will continue to share lessons learned as we travel together on the writer's way.

A special thank you to my proof-readers: Jonathan Bleier, Jacqui Penn, Elizabeth Wilmott, Karen Thomas, Heidi Uytendaal, Damian Cox and Alan Baxter.

Your feedback significantly helped shape the final version of the book. An extra thanks to Damian for the brilliant plot ideas and introducing me to the Preston & Child Pendergast series, which enabled me to see a future for Morgan's adventures.

Thank you to Tom Evans, TheBookWright.com who encouraged me to write fiction when I was blocked by the idea that I was only a non-fiction writer.

Also to Mur Lafferty whose advice "it's OK to suck with your first draft" helped me get the words down. The first draft of the novel was started during National Novel Writing Month (NaNoWriMo) and I would encourage any writer to participate if you want a jumpstart.

As an independent author in this process, I engaged a number of professionals along the way. Steve Parolini at TheNovelDoctor.com did a fantastic Editorial Review that helped me rejig the structure, plot and fill out the characters.

The cover was designed by Jane at JD Smith Design.

Thanks to Kristen Tate at The Blue Garret for editing the 2022 edition.